TRANS-GALACTIC BIKE RIDE

FEMINIST BICYCLE SCIENCE FICTION STORIES OF TRANSGENDER AND NONBINARY ADVENTURERS

EDITED BY

LYDIA ROGUE

ELLY BLUE PUBLISHING
PORTLAND, OR

TRANS GALACTIC BIKE RIDE
FEMINIST BICYCLE SCIENCE FICTION STORIES OF TRANSGENDER AND NONBINARY ADVENTURERS

Edited by Lydia Rogue

First printing, December 5, 2020

This is Microcosm #410
ISBN 9781621065081
Also available as an eBook 9781621061793

Elly Blue Publishing, an imprint of Microcosm Publishing
2752 N Williams Ave.
Portland, OR 97227

Cover by Cecila Granata
Design by Joe Biel

This is Bikes in Space Volume 7
For more volumes visit BikesInSpace.com
For more feminist bicycle books and zines visit TakingTheLane.com

Library of Congress Cataloging-in-Publication Data

Names: Blue, Elly, editor. | Rogue, Lydia, editor.
Title: Trans-galactic bike ride : feminist bicycle science fiction stories of transgender and nonbinary adventurers / edited by Elly Blue & Lydia Rogue.
Description: Portland, OR : Elly Blue Publishing, 2020. | Series: Bikes in space ; book 7 | Summary: "Take a ride with us as we explore a future where trans and nonbinary people are the heroes. In worlds where bicycle rides bring luck, a minotaur needs a bicycle, and werewolves stalk the post-apocalyptic landscape, nobody has time to question gender. Whatever your identity you'll enjoy these stories that are both thought-provoking and fun adventures. Find out what the future could look like if we stopped putting people into boxes and instead empowered each other to reach for the stars. Featuring brand-new stories from Hugo, Nebula, and Lambda Literary Award-winning author Charlie Jane Anders, Ava Kelly, Juliet Kemp, Rafi Kleiman, Tucker Lieberman, Nathan Alling Long, Ether Nepenthes, and Nebula-nominated M. Darusha Wehm. Also featuring debut stories from Diana Lane and Marcus Woodman"-- Provided by publisher.
Identifiers: LCCN 2020019866 | ISBN 9781621065081 (paperback) | ISBN 9781621061793 (epub)
Subjects: LCSH: Science fiction, American. | Transgender people--Fiction. | Gender-nonconforming people--Fiction. | Cycling--Fiction. | Feminist fiction, American.
Classification: LCC PS648.S3 T67 2020 | DDC 813/.0876208--dc23
LC record available at https://lccn.loc.gov/2020019866

Microcosm Publishing is Portland's most diversified publishing house and distributor with a focus on the colorful, authentic, and empowering. Our books and zines have put your power in your hands since 1996, equipping readers to make positive changes in their lives and in the world around them. Microcosm emphasizes skill-building, showing hidden histories, and fostering creativity through challenging conventional publishing wisdom with books and bookettes about DIY skills, food, bicycling, gender, self-care, and social justice. What was once a distro and record label was started by Joe Biel in his bedroom and has become among the oldest independent publishing houses in Portland, OR. We are a politically moderate, centrist publisher in a world that has inched to the right for the past 80 years.

Dedicated to anyone who ever looked for themself in vain on a bookshelf, so looked to the stars instead.

[CONTENTS]

INTRODUCTION

Introductions are hard. They're meant to tell the reader what to expect from the book, while being unimportant enough that someone who skips them doesn't miss out on any of the important content.

In this particular case, as with *True Trans Bike Rebel*, I found myself struggling with a bigger question: which reader do I talk to?

Do I talk to the reader this book is meant for—a small fraction of a percentage of humanity that is often overlooked or outright ignored—or do I talk to the reader who is more likely to be picking up this book—the privileged part of humanity that has been the focus of the speculative fiction genre for years? Do I talk to the new reader or do I talk to the person who's been following this series from the start?

Feminist bicycling science fiction is a niche genre at best. Add in a trans focus, and well…it's a niche that lives inside a niche. I've had a number of people ask me, in essence, "how many are you expecting to sell?"

The first time I was asked, I was floored—I'd never thought about it before. The book's existence was the point, and nothing more. (Of course, I also knew that it was going to be the 7th book in a series, so there was certainly a market!)

Right now, with all that's going on in the world, being able to exist is a challenge for trans folks. And while my goal with this book was to get it to exist, I wanted it to do more than that.

In one of the first submissions I got for this book, the author offered up proof of her 'qualifications.' "If you want proof, I can send you pictures of the pill bottles on my counter or a recording of me correctly pronouncing 'estradiol,'" she said.

I wasn't sure whether to laugh or cry.

I reassured her that I wasn't requiring "proof" (though I had a good chuckle when Elly Blue stumbled around attempting to pronounce estradiol, even as I mangle it half the time). So much of our lives is defined by the gatekeepers of society—whether it's demands that our bodies fit these specifications to be "male" or "female," therapists who want us to conform to gendered stereotypes and cis narratives of what it means to be trans, or even people in our own community who think there is only one way to be trans.

There was no way that this book was going to participate in that gatekeeping culture, so I pushed that this book was going to be by us, about us, and *for* us. The book should provide proof that there is a future beyond the now for us and that it will be beautiful.

With that as the framework, the submissions took on a beautiful shape. Rather than regurgitating the same narratives over and over again, we were allowed to tell our own narratives and find our own stories. By removing the cis gaze, it felt like we could breathe again.

So with that in mind, I invite you—whoever you are—to read this book. It may not be *for* you, but you are more than welcome to read it. Just remember that you are a guest in this house and that if you don't like it, there are millions of other books out there catered to you and your interests.

– Lydia Rogue

PER ROTAS AD ASTRA

Ether Nepenthes

Ember strapped the helmet beneath her chin and checked that her ears weren't peeking out in a weird way before pulling the visor down. The UI flickered before her eyes and the anarchist transgender pride flag filled her vision, bold letters proclaiming cheerfully that "GENDER IS OUR UNIVERSE." She stared at the "Initialisation Sequence" icon until her surroundings faded behind a blue filter and the countdown to launch.

She closed all non-essential communication channels, flexed her fingers around the handlebar grips, and settled down on her saddle. The protective force field spread around her with its usual buzz. Oxygen filled the air inside the force field, the tank icon appearing in the top left corner of her UI, and she winked twice towards it, then looked left three times in order to select the menthol flavour she fancied for this launch.

"So, uh. You're really doing this, aren't you?" Ash asked, xyr voice sounding a little higher through the headphones of Ember's helmet. "I mean, you ready for this?"

"Ash, I love you but your job right now is to give me atmospheric conditions," Ember answered, relaxing her shoulders. "Seventy-nine seconds to launch, I'm going to not change my mind *now*."

"Uh, everything's clear—all readings are holding steady. Everyone's texting me to say 'hi' and 'good luck' and things. Nathan says if you go 'round the shop, bring him snacks' I don't know what that means."

Ember chuckled. "Tell him he can go and ride his own space bike to the space shop. And get him a couple of Chocobars at InterMart use my account."

"Sure." A heartbeat. "Say, you've got—you've got your water, you've got your pills, you've got your rations, you, uh—"

"Ash." Ember sighed but forced herself to smile, because she'd been told people could actually hear the smile in one's voice. "It's fine, it's all fine. This isn't my first solo space trip, I'm not even the first disabled—"

"But you're the third," Ash protested. "And it is your first trip since surgery, and it's a bloody return trip, at that. To the *moon*."

"Listen, I got extra hot patches, extra meds, extra everything. It's like going camping, I just need to make sure I don't run out of oxygen. But that'll be easy without you to take my breath away."

"It's absolutely *not* like camping, and while that was very smooth, I'm still worried."

"Ash—"

"Yeah, I know. Back to work. Thirty seconds to launch."

"Thanks. Love you."

The countdown appeared at the low right corner of Ember's visor. She batted her eyelids and the initialisation sequence commands halved to a smaller window right above it, allowing her a clear view of the launching ramp. The bright red lights marking the upward curve she was meant to follow turned orange and she put her foot on the pedal.

"All right, we're sending you off," Ash said, not a wink later. "Take care and please get the voice channel back on as soon as you're out of orbit. Okay, so that's nine, eight, seven..."

The propulsion pad warmed up under Ember's other foot. She braced herself for launch, eyes fixed on the opening of starry night sky far up ahead.

"Six, five, four..."

She could feel the tremble in Ash's voice and the rumbles of the engines behind her. It was called a space bicycle because when the momentum would stop propelling her forwards, she would have to pedal her way through in order to supplement the energy gathered from the stellar panels spread all over the vehicle. Low gravity would do the rest. Space bikes had been invented to circumvent an old transportation law. A space bike even had wheels, for launch and landing; it was possible to ride it on most of the known planets, technically, but the sturdy and thus burdensome hull and the requirements of both gravity and stellar energy were such that it would not make much sense to. Ember didn't ride hers anywhere other than in space or around the training centre. She had non-spatial, regular bikes for her non-spatial, regular travels, after all.

"...three, two, one...Zero—See you, babe!"

“Love you!” Ember shouted over the shock wave that sent her up the launching ramp. “Ember December, on my way to the moon!”

She shut off the voice channel and tightened her grip on the handlebar. She couldn’t help but start pedalling now, even if she knew she was losing precious stamina for nothing at all—and that this was the reason she’d settled for the silver medal in the first ever long-distance bicycle race back in 2386, and hadn’t that been the most frustrating thing?—but it was a habit.

Soon the ramp faded from her sight, replaced by the velvet-like black of the desert night. Space cyclists of yore used to have to follow cables and ramps all the way, rendering long-distance trips like this one impossible; but Ember hadn’t gotten a MoonoCross with enhanced venusian stabilisers just to follow a traced road. She’d fallen in love with biking because it allowed her to get off the roads and into the woods and mountains. Of course, a space trip implied following a strictly defined route, sleeping cycles, and meal times, but the only communication channels available up there were the launch centre and Ash’s personal cell, and that was *priceless*.

With an average speed of 2,000 km per hour thanks to her own inertia as the only resistance and an approximate distance of 350,000 km thanks to the moon being at its perigee, it would take Ember roughly six and a half days to reach her planned landing site.

Six and a half days of pure solitary bliss, the great void of night, nothing to see but the stars, the Earth getting smaller and smaller behind her, the moon herself slowly closing in. Ember knew this sort of trip would drive so many of her friends mad, but to her it was very much the point.

This was why she loved biking so much, she thought as she glanced back to the twinkling lights of the launch centre below. She liked to take her time and admire the view along the way. She liked that she could ride along with others and on her own. She liked the physicality of it, the feeling of her feet pedalling faster and faster without so much as breaking a sweat as she switched gear after gear.

She liked that whether on Earth or in space, biking would lead her to places others might have travelled before her, but which still felt like hers to discover. Whether it was a hidden brook or an asteroid too small to be charted, there wasn't much difference to her. Her bike would ride her into the great unknown—and then back home.

RIDING FOR LUCK

Juliet Kemp

Some days the tarmac unrolls smooth under your wheels, and every light goes green for you. Some days the pedals spin like your legs aren't even trying, smooth like this is what you were built for.

Some days you lean around the corner and rise out of the saddle, like god herself is slinging you round.

Some days, if you just kept pedalling, there's something just out of reach, something you can nearly catch...

...and then you brake, and you slow, and you stop; and it's school or work or home just like usual, the feeling bleeding right on out of you like it was never even there.

Was it ever there?

• • •

The first time I rode into the luck, it was an accident. It was one of those days when everything just goes your way, when the bike feels like part of you and every light goes green and the gaps open up as if by magic. Of course, at the time I was assuming that it wasn't. Magic, that is.

I got all the way from home to Soho without having to put my foot down once. It was glorious. When I stopped, I could feel the fizz in my fingers. I thought it was just pleasure in something satisfying, a sort of achievement of the stars aligning. It never occurred to me that my sense of banked power might be real and not just the rush of self-satisfaction.

I was meeting someone, an online hookup, and it went better than any date I'd been on in months. We hit it off like we had chatting online. She laughed at all of my jokes. The whole evening soaked in that joy of feeling like everything just slides into place, like you're wholly on form, being who you want to be. A glorious date. And a glorious evening thereafter, as it happens. And I never thought about the matter of the luck. Why would I?

• • •

The relationship didn't last, though we parted friends. I didn't know, then, about the luck, but I did remember how that non-stop ride felt, and even though I hadn't realised what it meant, I wanted to repeat the feeling.

I started paying attention to traffic light sequences, started looking further ahead to slip past traffic without stopping. And, slowly, I began to notice how it felt, after a successful run. Something electric-slippery that ran over my skin, that sparked in my fingertips, after a successful run. Something that led to changes—just tiny ones—in my day. The creaky lift in my current office being there when I needed it instead of having to wait five minutes. Discount brownies at the coffee shop. My phone battery lasting just those couple of minutes that I needed to find out which pub my friends were in. Little things that felt like luck. Like I could ride myself into luck, absurd though I told myself that was.

And then, too, there were the things that weren't exactly luck. Things like someone asking for my pronouns at my next temp job (which never, ever happens). Things like being neither 'sir'-ed nor 'madam'-ed at a restaurant. Things I didn't want to think of as luck because they ought to be normal, except for how they're not. Little things that felt like a massive difference.

I started to wonder. But it didn't feel like something I could believe in. Not really. I mean, like I say. It was absurd, right?

I'd been at it for a couple of months, still not allowing myself to believe in it, when I saw Elin for the first time. She sailed past me when I'd been caught by traffic lights, slowing just enough to stay the right side of the lights until they changed, then accelerating away through the junction. Her pink-and-black braids were wound up in a loose bun on the back of her head, and her legs, in leggings under a bright blue skirt, were incredible. (I try not to be that shallow, but sometimes you just notice, right? And I'd just upped my dose of T. These things were on my mind.) I tried to catch her, but she went through the next lights just before they turned red, and I wasn't close enough to follow. I watched her zip down the street, and I wondered.

I saw her again in the same place a couple of days later, but this time I had my timing right too, and we paced each other all the way along the road. Finally we got stuck behind a lorry, and had to stop. She looked over at me, and my fingertips sparked, and we both grinned, suddenly, knowing, even if I still couldn't quite bring myself to believe it.

"Elin," she said.

"Kell," I said.

"You know the Oak, on Portland Place?" she asked. "Sunday evening. You should come."

And then the lorry moved and she nodded at me and took off down a side-street.

• • •

I wondered for the rest of the week whether or not I should go to the Oak. Maybe this was all just blatant absurdity and I was conning myself on to think that there was anything going on here; that this person had looked at me, meaningfully.

But then, even if all she wanted was for me to hang out with other cyclists, wouldn't that be worth going anyway? (I considered, briefly, optimistically, then discarded, the thought that she might have been coming onto me. I hadn't got that vibe. Unfortunately.)

So, yeah. I went to the Oak, that Sunday.

I spent most of the ride there freaking out about the whole gender/pronouns thing. I hate 'coming out', but if I don't, I get read a certain way. And if I do, there's always the risk that I say my pronouns and it turns out that I'm introducing myself to transphobic shitheads. But. The reason I knew the Oak already was that it had bloody great big Pride flags outside the windows. And I had my bike. If I needed to leave, I could just...do it. I was trying to be more confident, more sure in myself, in my sense of who I was. I would damn well introduce myself like that.

I deliberately slowed for the lights, on the way over, deliberately put a foot down. I didn't want to wonder if this thing, this thing that surely had to be imaginary, was affecting how these particular people reacted to me. I didn't want to risk it changing, after.

When I got there, the racks outside the pub were festooned with bikes; I had to lock up to some railings down the way. I took it as a good sign. I saw Elin as soon as I walked into the place: those pink-and-black braids, the light shining off her dark skin. She was in the corner by the bar. I swallowed hard and walked over.

"Oh, hey! Awesome! You came."

She stuck out the hand that wasn't holding her beer, and, cautiously, I took it.

"Like I said before. I'm Elin. She pronouns."

I felt a surge of relief, overwhelming to the point that my knees shook. "Kell. Uh. They pronouns."

She smiled at me, and turned to introduce me to the other two people standing with her. Cara and Flora—both she. I went to get myself a pint, and came back to find Cara in the middle of a story about "some dick in a Beemer" who had yelled at her when she was cycling over here.

"And then inevitably I find myself wondering—are they being a shit because I'm a woman, because I'm a cyclist, or because I'm trans?"

"Embrace the power of 'and'," Flora said, dry as bone, and all of us laughed, that laughter you get when you all know the score.

I've rarely settled into a group so fast. It was an evening of connection, of shared experience. And at the end, as the staff were calling time at the bar, Elin looked over at me.

"Hey. Kell. Wanna come for a ride with us?" She grinned, slightly sideways. "Evening's a good time for it."

My blood sang. I nodded.

• • •

Cara led. Away from the Oak and out along the main road, until Elin shouted to her, "When are you going to call it?"

We passed through a set of traffic lights.

"Now," Cara said, and something crackled between the four of us.

Elin gestured me up to ride beside her, two abreast behind Cara and Flora.

"Easier to keep together this way," she said.

Cara knew what she was about. We went through the first set of lights on green, accelerated to catch the next ones, then slowed so that by the time we reached set three, they'd gone from red to red-and-amber and we could sail straight through. Set four went red as we rode up towards them, and I thought we'd lost it, until Cara signalled left and dove down a side street. Now we were winding our way through the backstreets, swift but steady, Cara calling "clear!" as she made each turn. I couldn't stop myself from grinning as that feeling, the feeling of balancing on something perfect, spread through my body. From the look on Elin's face when I glanced over at her, it was clear that she felt it too.

"To Mare Street," Cara called back to us, and rode on.

She got us all the way to Mare Street without a single stop, and the wild joy was rising in my blood as I followed her and Flora into a deserted carpark outside what looked like a doctor's surgery, and we all stopped.

I nearly fell over as my foot touched the floor, the shock zinging through me and tingling in my teeth. I couldn't not believe it any more. Not with the three of them here with me, sharing it. Not when I felt it that strongly.

"Woo!" Cara put her head back and whooped at the night sky.

"That should see me through tomorrow," Flora said.

Elin was looking at me, exuberant and just slightly questioning. I nodded back at her and her grin spread wider.

"It's pretty good, huh?"

We all grinned at each other like loons, like moons, like cyclists.

"Welcome to the club," Elin said, and hugged me.

• • •

We met up every week. And gathered notes in-between times, working out our own routes, competing to be the one who'd managed the longest during the week. You had to call a route in advance for it to work best, the others told me. And you had to have an intention; you couldn't just call the end when you hit a snag.

Daytime was more challenging. Daytime runs won you more points, in our unspoken competition. But you got the same amount of—power, luck, rightness, whatever you cared to call it—either way, so the longer the run, the better it was to do it at night. Night meant longer light timings, less traffic to get in the way, and fewer suicidal pedestrians. Sunday evenings were the best; weekdays a close second. Fridays and Saturdays the streets were always full of wankers and idiots, drunk or showing off or both.

We took turns leading, on a Sunday evening. It seemed to me like the four of us together made it more than riding alone.

"You know," Elin said, once. "I've been wondering if we shouldn't do something with it."

"Speak for yourself," Cara said. "I do stuff with it. I filled my prescription last Monday. First time they've ever got it right first time without faffing around."

"Mm," Elin said. "But something…more. Bigger."

We didn't pursue it further. Not then.

The week things changed, Flora turned up late, and miserable.

"The squat's being evicted tomorrow," she said.

"The centre?" Cara asked. "Where I ran that gender group?"

"Where I did the bike-mechanic thing?" Elin asked at the same time.

Flora nodded.

"Ah, shit. Fuck 'em. No chance of a reprieve?"

Flora shrugged. "We'll rally tomorrow, try and see the bailiffs off, but..." We all knew how squat evictions went. "We were about to go to court, and Dolly reckons we've got a good chance, but if they get us out before that..."

And just like that, I got the idea.

"Our ride tonight," I said, slowly, trying to think it through. "Is there any way we could, somehow...pass it on? What happens?"

The others stared at me.

"I have literally no idea," Elin said. "I've only ever used it for myself."

Cara's eyes were wide. "I did. Once. For a friend who was waiting to hear about his gender recognition certificate. Rode to where I was meeting him. Hugged him as my feet touched the ground. He had such a go at me for riding into him, cos I didn't dare explain, but..."

"Did it work?" Flora asked, urgently.

Cara shrugged. "It didn't feel like I got anything myself. And he got his GRC. So. Maybe?"

We all looked at one another.

"Well," Elin said, finally. "It's worth a go. Right?"

• • •

We never usually planned out routes, not on paper, but this one felt like we had to think it out in advance. We needed something big, surely, to get enough of an impact, and all the routes we knew individually didn't seem like they'd be enough. We had to do something else. Pull the pieces of the city together.

Huddled around the pub table trying to work out how to do it, we realised fairly quickly that tiny maps on phone screens weren't going to cut it. Cara went to the service station up the road and got an A-to-Z and a biro. Old school. We marked out all the routes we knew, between us, around the squat—and realised that we could link them up, and create a loop, starting and finishing at the squat.

"Circles," Cara said. "Circles have to be stronger, right?"

The bell rang for time at the bar. Ten thirty—the Oak kept traditional Sunday hours. Normally we weren't in much of a hurry to leave, but tonight…

"Right then," Elin said, standing up. "Let's go."

• • •

I didn't want the responsibility of leading. None of us did. We all stood there outside the squat, once we'd got there, for a moment, looking at one another, holding our bikes, the tension in the air but not going anywhere.

"Take turns," Cara said, her chin going up slightly. "That's the fairest way, right?" She turned to Flora. "You should finish. The last section. You're the one most linked to the squat."

The trouble was, all of this was sympathetic magic, was us making it up as we went along, going only by what we thought made sense and by what had happened before and by the pricking of our thumbs. It might make no difference at all if we did it this way. It might make no difference at all if we did it at all. Sure, Cara said she'd been able to transfer the whatever-it-was—the power, the luck, whatever—but that was to a person, not to an institution, and she wasn't even really sure it had happened.

We had to try, though. Right?

"I'll start," I said abruptly, wanting suddenly to be doing something, moving things along. "I know that bit of the route best." It was true, even.

"I'll take second," Cara said. "Elin, you okay with third?"

I clipped my foot into my pedal, then pulled it up to set the pedal properly, and squared my shoulders. The lights on the main road were red, and I glanced at the others to make sure they were all ready.

The lights went red-and-amber.

"Come on then," I said, pushing down on the pedal. "Let's go."

The first section was easy enough. Arguably it was a bit like cheating, then, for me to take it, but it was also true enough that it was the bit I knew best. North up the road from the squat, straight through those first lights, then in the daytime you could catch the next set clear, but at this time of night you only got them once in two rounds, and I hadn't been able to see which round they were on from in front of the squat. I went to the backstreets instead, left and right and left again, the others following behind me. I slowed to let a taxi go past at the next junction, then slotted us in behind it.

Up ahead, the crossing lights went red, and the pedestrian beep sounded. We all slowed, slowed further; this wasn't a long cycle, it should be fine. Flashing amber again, but I'd seen the next lights go red, so I kept our slow pace until we were almost on them, and they were going red-amber as we accelerated again through them.

One more left turn, back into the side streets, and it was Cara's turn now. She had the Old Street roundabout, a bugger of a connection, but she timed it perfectly, sweeping three-quarters of the way round and peeling off again despite the boy-racer type who tried to cut us up halfway through. Synchronised, without thinking about it, we all gave him the finger at once as he gunned his engine and raced away. Arsehole.

Elin's section we nearly lost it; not her fault. Some drunk idiot pedestrian dived out in front of her without looking. She swerved around them—we all did, just about, and Flora swore at him—but it cost us a couple of seconds, and that was it, we'd lost the next lights. That one was always a close connection. I saw Elin begin to panic, and called out, "There's a right up ahead, before the lights."

A right, but also a steady stream of traffic coming the other way, against us. We all slowed, slowed again, to the point of wobbling, all desperately trying to stay aboard. Elin found a gap in the traffic and shot across, Flora with her. I went for it, much closer than I really should have done, and earnt myself a justified hoot from the irate driver.

"Shit, shit," I heard from behind me, and looked back to see Cara, foot down, shaking her head.

"Go on! I'll catch you there!"

Would it still work, with just three of us, if four had started out?

No way of finding out other than to keep going, to see it through.

"We dropped Cara," I said, once I'd caught the other two up. "She says, keep going."

"My turn," Flora said, grimly. "Come on then. Last sprint."

And suddenly, everything was smooth, falling into place like molten gold, like that moment when you're flying and nothing can stop you. Lights changed for us, I swear; at least twice I thought we'd had it but then the three of us sailed serenely through, moving like a single entity. My bike seemed to thrum underneath me.

Last corner, holding back the urge to rejoice already.

"Shit!" That was Flora, up ahead, and my heart sank.

A giant lorry was reversing, slowly and with much beeping (at this time of night? The neighbours would be steaming) into the building site a few doors down from the squat. And blocking the entire road whilst doing so. We exchanged glances, slowed. It was moving, moving; but too slow. We slowed further, almost to stopping, as a tiny gap opened between lorry and kerb, right over on the wrong side of the road.

I saw the tiny shift of Flora's weight in the saddle as she made up her mind. She dived across the road, pedals flying, skidded around the end of the lorry, and without letting myself think too much about it, I followed suit. I skimmed the bumper of the car on the other side, patiently waiting its turn, grimaced apologetically at the driver—we weren't doing any favours for the image of cyclists tonight—and heard Elin swearing as she followed suit. The lorry inched further forwards. The car started moving just after Elin cleared its bumper. I could see Cara already standing in the yard in front of the squat, jumping up and down. I was right on Flora's tail now, and she slewed left into the driveway of the squat, rode right up to the wall, and braked hard. She fell sideways onto it, and I followed straight after her, like we'd been riding team pursuit at some velodrome somewhere, Flora, me, Elin, one two three.

I fell against the wall, hitting my shoulder hard, and my head rang like a bell. I felt everything that had been building up inside me drain away, the fizz in my fingers fizzing its way out through my skin and...somewhere. To the building? Did that even make sense?

I unclipped my right foot and let it touch the floor, then my left, and collapsed over my handlebars. I felt unbelievably weary, far more than was in any way reasonable after what we'd just ridden. Behind me, I could hear Elin's breath coming hard.

"Fantastic," Cara said. "You did it. Sorry I dropped."

"Better dropped than squashed," I said. "Which was nearly what happened to me, so."

"That last bit around the lorry was amazing," Cara said. "You all just appeared around the corner of it like, I dunno, fucking Valkyries or something."

"Furies," Elin said. "Riding for justice."

"Please tell me no one's murdered anyone," I said, which seemed funny enough to make me giggle out loud at myself.

"Do you think it's worked, though?" Elin asked the question we were all wondering.

Flora sighed. "Dunno. I guess we'll find out tomorrow."

"If there's any justice in the world…" Cara said darkly.

"Well. If there is, I guess we tried to summon it," Flora said, and smiled at us all, looking more than exhausted herself. "Thanks, all of you. I appreciate it."

Whatever happened now, at least we'd tried.

"If it's worked, though," Cara said, thoughtfully, "if it's worked… What next?"

We looked around at each other, daring to be hopeful. I felt that spark in my fingers again, felt a smile creeping onto my face, saw the same expression on the others.

Well. It's not like I haven't always known that bikes can change the fucking world.

THE EDGE OF THE ABYSS

M. Darusha Wehm

A version of the story first appeared in *Contact Light*, edited by Megan Chee and Ron Garner. Silence in the Library, LLC. 2015

I'd just settled into a comfortable pedalling pace when the radio crackled to life. I sighed. It was probably one of the local wits passing me and unable to keep their clever thought contained. "Get off the trajectory, you hippie," was a classic. "Buy a generator," was another one I heard frequently, as if it had never occurred to me to switch up my custom crank-powered personal starrunner to the stock fission-drive model you could see mouldering away at auction lots across the quadrant. Maybe this would be my personal favourite: the heart's-in-the-right-place, "Want a tow?"

I couldn't ignore the scratchy bip-bipping of the radio's notification. I forced myself to slow down to a leisurely pace and thumbed the comms. "This is Starlite Blue, go ahead."

My shoulder muscles loosened when I heard the gruff voice come though the tinny speaker. "April, my dear, what brings you to this part of the universe?"

Usually it drove me crazy when people didn't bother with proper radio protocol, but I could forgive Admiral Grant anything. He wasn't a real Admiral, had never been in anyone's military as far as I knew, but he was the sweetest old space dog I'd ever met, and it was the only name he'd ever given me.

"Switch to channel seven-two, sir," I suggested to get us off the working channel. The Admiral could get away with anything but there was a limit to how far I'd join him in radio anarchy.

"Roger," he said and, after a quick thumb stroke of my transceiver, we were back in business. "So, what brings you all the way out to this patch of sky?" Grant asked. "I'm sure I'd have heard about it if there was your kind of work 'round here."

I smiled as my legs got back into an easy rhythm. Grant sounded like a bluff old space captain who had about as much discretion as a green marine fresh off the vomit comet, but I knew better. We weren't in exactly the same racket—the Admiral traded in goods whereas I delivered information. Nothing overtly illegal in most of the jurisdictions where we operated, but not something you spoke about on the open comms, either.

"I'm not here for work," I answered. "I'm on holiday."

The laugh that came over the speaker nearly shook me off my saddle. "Who in heavens comes all the way out to this neck of the woods for a holiday? What are you looking for, an unobstructed view of dark matter?"

It's true, the Sigma system isn't exactly a classic tourist destination. Once the Cyndex asteroid mining operations cleared out, most of the people moved on to places with more work or more fun. I wasn't looking for excitement though.

"You could say that," I answered Grant. "I think of it as the call of the sea, the lure of the open road."

"Ahh," Grant said. "You're all the way out here to get away from the traffic."

I laughed. I hadn't thought about it that way, but he was right enough. There were settlements close enough here that I could resupply and rest when I needed to, but the direct trajectories were relatively free of other ships. It was, in short, a really nice route for a cycler.

"So where are you putting in?" Grant asked.

"I'll be at Cyndex Colony Two in—" I glanced at the nav station's projected ETA, "fourteen standard hours, give or take."

"Why don't I stop by," Grant said, "let a lady buy me a drink?"

"You aren't on deadline?" I asked.

"Not this time," Grant said, "I was looking for an excuse to stop."

"It's a date," I said. "Starlite Blue clear." I thumbed off the comms and eyed the battery monitor. Another hour and I'd be topped off for the rest of the trip to Cyndex. I turned the book I was reading back on and let my legs do the work.

• • •

I remembered when Bao's was the most happening gin joint in the sector. Rowdy, sure. Barfights, there were a few. But mostly it was full of miners getting their R&R in every way imaginable. I saw things going on in full view of everyone in the place that I'd only ever read about in dirty books.

Now, the bar was clean, the chairs scarred but intact, and getting a table was guaranteed. They said that almost 90% of the folks on Cyndex Two left once the mining operation closed and the ones who stayed were mainly family-first types and the odd adventurer. It was the latter group who managed to keep Bao's running, along with folks like me and the Admiral who stopped by on our way someplace else.

The owner was running the bar when I walked in and their eyes fell on me like hungry wolves. "April May," Bao said, their rough voice croaking out the syllables of my name, "it has been too long. What'll it be?"

I looked past the ancient barkeep to the beer fridge and saw nothing but the nondescript green of Steinie bottles. I grimaced. "Anything more interesting in the back?"

Bao smiled, which did nothing to make them look any less terrifying. "I've got a few Paulie's stouts; for you—two for one." I knew that meant one bottle would cost the same as two Steinies, but that wasn't completely unreasonable. I nodded, wondering how much trouble it was to get around the sanctions and bring in the Paulie's.

I poured my drink into the glass Bao handed me and wondered some more. I had no illusions about the work I did. In another time or another place it would be called espionage, maybe treason. Even now it wasn't exactly the kind of thing you talked about openly when someone asked, "So, what do you do?"

But the right of individuals to pursue their own interests was about the only thing that the Liberty Alliance and the Progressive Free State agreed on, so they couldn't stop the transfer of information, technology, and goods between their spheres of influence. They just made it difficult, which gave people like me plenty of work.

I was thinking about the bits of info I'd stashed away from the last job I'd been on, when I heard the unmistakable voice of Admiral Grant. "Bao!" he said, his voice carrying all the way from the corridor. "How have you been, you old reprobate?"

I looked up and saw Bao grinning like a skeleton. "Much better since I last saw the back of you, Grant." He laughed in a way that made me wonder about the precise nature of his relationship with Bao. He walked over to the bar, taking in the whole room at a glance. He looked much the same as the last time I'd seen him about a year previously. The same long gray hair roughly tied at the base of his head and the same tunic that looked like it might have once been part of a uniform but was so discoloured with age and wear that its origin was unrecognizable. The casual observer could easily be mistaken in thinking that the Admiral neglected his appearance, if not for his neatly trimmed and waxed moustache.

"Get me a wine, would you?" he said while slipping into the seat across from me. "April, look at you. You must be twice the size you were the last time I saw you."

I laughed. "They do wonders with muscle mass over at the Proxima spas."

Grant whistled. "You look different every time I see you. Business must be good."

I nodded and took a sip of my beer. "The day I stop changing is the day you know I've finally gotten old."

"I've never gotten into modding," he said, "but they say it can be addictive."

"I'm just keeping up with the tech," I said, and he raised an eyebrow. "But, yeah, I've been at it a while."

"When did you start?" We'd never really talked about our pasts before, but he seemed interested, and it beat talking about which brand of hull paint we liked.

"I got my first tech mod when I was fourteen, but I'd been on hormone blockers since I was twelve. I've always been a self-made woman."

He nodded. "Fourteen sounds about right."

"Yeah, it is now. It wasn't much of a mod, just a screen implant that kids nowadays get from Santa, but back then..." I sighed. I hadn't told this story in a long time, but something in Grant's eyes made me talkative. Or maybe it was something in the Paulie's.

"The neighbours called a Child Protection company in. It was awful—they accused my parents of abuse, of turning me into a machine. I didn't understand it at the time, but now I think it wasn't just the tech that bothered them. When I changed my name they didn't even try to get it right for nearly a year. At least they called a decent protection outfit. The guy they sent out took one look at me and dismissed the complaint. But the neighbours... ugh, it was hard putting up with their disgusted looks all the time. I was so happy when they left."

"They weren't part of the Morality Rebellion, were they? Those people who protested when the Alliance government came in?"

"We never called it that, but yeah. And it wasn't the government they were upset about exactly. More like the loosening of restrictions on personal choice that came with the Alliance. They just couldn't handle seeing other people doing things they didn't approve of. It was ugly for a while, but they were outnumbered. Ultimately, it was like it or leave it, so most of them left."

"They're the ones who founded the outer colonies, aren't they?"

I shrugged. "That's what they say. I've got no plans to go see for myself, that's for sure. Seems to me it worked out for everyone. They get their pristine communities with their rules and regulations and the rest of us don't have to put up with a bunch of interventionist reactionaries. Win-win." I took a sip of my beer. "Speaking of rebellions, I heard there was a border crackdown over in the Shankar system. Cargoes seized, rumours of someone getting jumpy with a laser gun."

Grant nodded, all traces of jocularity gone. "For once the rumours are true," he said. "It was a pal of mine at the receiving end."

"Bad?" I said.

Grant nodded. "Third-degree burns with complications. Onboard medlab couldn't hack it."

"I'm so sorry," I said.

Grant didn't say anything more, and I didn't know what to say to that. I'd heard the smuggler's ship was giving off a Progressive energy signature and the Alliance patrol shot at it. Not standard operating procedure, but no one in Alliance Command would lose sleep over it. Still, even though hostilities between the Progressives and the Alliance were loud and proud, casualties weren't common.

Bao arrived with a large glass of wine, which they placed wordlessly next to Grant's left hand. They let their hand drop to his shoulder and I saw the slightest hint of a squeeze, then they were gone.

He took a deep draught then said, "Here's to all of us out here scraping by in the big black, caught between two monsters."

I lifted my pint glass in his direction. "To the ones who've gone before." We clicked our glasses, drank, and let the silence descend for a while.

• • •

Grant told me he was staying overnight at the station, and I'd planned to be there a few days, so we agreed to meet the next day before he left. I'd hired the use of a guest room—my cycler was my home but it was small, and if I were on a vacation I might as well be able to take a bath. I'd turned off all my devices before crawling into the soft bed, all alarms and alerts forced silent. I woke after a deep sleep to the pleasant glow of the station's artificial sun. I'd picked out one of the few restaurants for breakfast and after getting dressed opened the door of my quarters to a scene of utter chaos.

Cyndex Two wasn't anywhere near as populated as it had been when the mining operation in the nearby asteroid belt was running, but there were still several thousand people living there. And every last one of them seemed to be running down the corridor outside my room.

I tried to stop a man who nearly crashed into me, but he shrugged off my arm and ignored my questions. "What's going on?" I asked again, more loudly this time, in the hopes that someone, anyone, might answer. Someone who bore the characteristic stoop of a lifelong miner stepped out of the river of people to stand beside me.

"Looks like there's finally going to be a shooting war," the ex-miner said. "Turns out the Alliance installed a military outpost just at the edge of the Nune colony. It just came online."

"An outpost?" I asked, thinking that Nune was huge, the main Progressive colony. Millions lived there.

My source nodded. "One of the new Protector class stations. A thousand fighters, they say."

"What are they thinking?" I asked, not expecting an answer.

"News feeds say it's to protect the research labs in the Altera sector." The miner looked at me. "Where you from?" Cyndex was independent, so the people living there could have held allegiance to either or neither of the two major powers. It never really seemed to matter out here.

"All over," I said, "but I'm an Alliance citizen." I got a curt nod in return, but I noticed some of the tension went out of the conversation.

"They say that research station is really important, something to do with extending the range of energy cells. I guess they have to do something to make sure it stays out of Progressive hands."

I nodded, even if I didn't really buy the theory. "This is bad," I said, "but what's with the panic? Altera's nowhere near here."

"You didn't know? The station's been locked down," the miner said. "No one in or out. Word is that it's just a matter of time before the Progressive trigger fingers get itchy and they try to remove the Altera outpost by force. They say those Protector stations can take out a lot of matter in a single strike. It's going to get ugly and it isn't going to be contained."

"Yeah," I said. "Thanks." I turned to fight my way against the flow of people to try and find Grant.

He was from Nune.

• • •

He wasn't in the guest quarters section, but I wasn't surprised. I only looked there because it was on the way to docking. I knew he'd be on his ship.

I hit the ship's bell on the hull and waited. It wasn't long before until I heard the squeal of someone undogging the hatch and the heavy outer airlock door opened. "You heard the news," he said, inscrutable. He stood back allowing me just enough room to get through the hatch. "Probably treason just talking to you," he said, "you might as well come in."

I smiled, but somehow our usual banter wasn't fun anymore. I guess because all those jokes about being on opposite sides were no longer just jokes. I stepped into his ship and jumped when the airlock door banged shut. I turned to face Grant and said, "If I'd known anything about this..."

He stopped me with a wave of his hand. "No one saw this coming," he said, "no one outside the inner circles anyway. I'm as clued in to the scuttlebutt as you, my dear, and I hadn't even heard a peep." He passed me as he started walking down the passage. I fell into step behind him, only a tiny part of my mind screaming at me to get off this ship as soon as possible. The rest of me knew that even if Grant was a Progressive, he was still the only friend I had in this sector. Maybe the quadrant.

"For all the freedoms we enjoy," he said as he opened a door set into the bulkhead, "freedom of information isn't exactly one of them." He turned and gestured for me to climb the ladder on the other side of the door. When I emerged through the gap in the deck I could see into a small, but comfortable sitting room-style cockpit. I made my way up the rest of the companionway and walked over to the small settee. I had an unobstructed 360º view out the flybridge. There were more ships docked here than I'd realized.

"It's no different on my side," I said when Grant appeared at the top of the companionway. "I'd be out of a job if it were." He laughed and for a moment he looked like the Grant I'd always known, but then it passed.

"Drink?" he asked.

"Definitely." He took down a bottle of something thick and dark and poured us two large measures. He handed me a glass and paused a moment before clinking his with mine.

"Cheers," he said.

"Indeed," I answered. The drink went down rough. "It's a bit early for me," I said, catching my breath.

Grant cackled. "What else are you going to do trapped on a dying, nominally independent colony world on the eve of galactic armageddon?" he said.

I laughed and took another, smaller, sip. "Drinking before noon doesn't seem like that much of a problem when you put it that way," I said. Grant settled into the armchair across from me and peered into his glass.

"It's bad for business," he said, finally. "Bad for business and bad for that holiest-of-holies, individual liberty. Both sides must realize that, surely."

I nodded. The Alliance was founded on the principles of an unfettered marketplace, of the right of all citizens to be free from state interference in their personal and business lives. The news feeds back home made it sound like the Progressives were practically communists, but I knew that was propaganda.

"They're too much alike, our two sides," I said. "Sometimes I think that's why we fight."

Grant snorted. "The only difference is we think the state is for schools and hospitals and you think it's for cops and armies, right?"

I smiled. "It's not that simple and you know it," I said.

"No, but it's close enough."

A flash of light caught my eye and as I turned to look out the viewport I heard the explosion. "What the hell?"

"Looks like folks are getting restless," Grant said. I could see that one of the docked ships had fired on the docking clamps keeping it moored—and its crew trapped—at the station. All they'd done was damage their ship, making it harder for them to leave when the lockdown was over. Assuming total war didn't break out and we all started killing each other.

"Sometimes I wonder if a bit of regulation might not be such a bad thing," I said, "keep the idiots out of my patch of space."

Grant turned away from the viewport and walked back over to the drinks cabinet. "They'd still manage to sneak though," he said. "Fewer, probably, but there's no stopping idiocy." He poured another measure and held the bottle up to me. I nodded and he brought it with him to the settee. He topped off my glass and sat.

"It's a strange life for people like us," he said, staring out the viewport. "Most folks never leave the gravity well where they were born, never actually meet anyone from the other side. People like you and me, the folks out here at the edges, we see it all more clearly."

"See what?"

"The blurred lines, the shades of grey." He lifted his glass and drained half the contents. "The price of fucking freedom." He laughed—a terrible sound—and it dawned on me that he'd had a bit of a head start on the drinking. I couldn't blame him—I'd always thought that if either the Alliance or the Progressives got hot weapons anywhere near the other side, the best we could hope for was a long, ugly war. More likely was a few minutes of madness, then flames and murder and survivors who envied the dead.

"You have family on Nune?" I asked.

He nodded. "We aren't close. I left for a reason. But they don't deserve what's coming. No one does."

There wasn't anything to say; he was right. I reached for the bottle and he passed it over.

• • •

I don't know how much later it was when I woke on the settee in Grant's ship, a few black patches in my memory. I was okay with that. I did a little deep breathing to activate my adrenaline production, then when the nausea passed got up and looked around the ship. Grant was gone.

I undogged the hatch and stepped out into the docking level. I stuck my head out the door, but the chaos was over. The hallway wasn't deserted, but at least no one was panicking any more. I made my way to the main hall in the hopes of finding Grant or news or food. Especially food. My magic muscles go through protein like a star cruiser eats fuel, and I was running on low.

I heard the sounds of people and saw that most of the station was in there, an Alliance broadcast on the screen. I looked around until I saw a food cart and followed my grumbling stomach. I ordered some noodles with double tofu and scanned the room as I waited. I hadn't seen so many people in Cyndex's hall since the mines were open. Grant was at a corner table with Bao, the two watching the broadcast in silence.

"Hey," the noodle guy said, bringing my attention back home. I thanked him and took my bowl over to a nearby table. I wedged myself between a couple of people staring at the news screen and began shoveling the food into my mouth. As I ate, I watched the news, too.

"...entering the twenty-seventh hour of the Seige of Nune." The pretty talking head on the Alliance feed was wearing what I thought of as Grim Expression Number Two, and they'd ginned up a flashy logo for the ticker than ran under the computer-generated face. It was a wonder what people thought of the universe if this was the only way they got information. "The military has dispatched its full arsenal to patrol the borders of the Nune Colony and all active duty personnel have been recalled to their bases. Our team embedded with the Fourteenth Spaceborne Artillery are reporting that a preemptive strike against the occupying Progressive force on the edge of Nune space has not been ruled out as a possibility. Military leaders are unable to share anything more at this time."

My tipped-up noodle bowl was obscuring my view, so I didn't see what happened next, but I heard a voice across from me say, "Typical Alliance bastards, just looking for an excuse to invade sovereign space."

"We're not the ones with a thousand fighters occupying territory on the edge of your largest colony," the woman on my left said, her voice quivering. I could hear similar arguments breaking out around the room.

"Come on," I said, putting my bowl down. "Things are different out here. You're both miners, right?" They each nodded. "You've got way more in common with each other than any of us do with folks on the main colonies. Who cares if you're from the Alliance and you're Progressive? It's all just an accident of birth, anyway. What's the point in letting a bunch of politicos turn us against each other?"

"No one out here with any sense has any love for the Alliance," the guy across from me said. "Cyndex left us all high and dry when they pulled out of the mines, and it was the Alliance and their damned 'noninterference' that allowed it to happen. They let companies get away with murder. It's the only reason Cyndex incorporated in Alliance territory."

"Oh, come on," the woman said, "if it weren't for the Progressive government's repressive corporate oversight, companies like Cyndex wouldn't have to cut and run as soon as they took a little hit on their bottom line. If you're going to blame anyone for Cyndex leaving, blame the lazy bastards getting free drugs on Nune."

"That's it!" The short guy across from me was quicker than he looked—he leapt across the table. He was aiming for the woman, and I instinctively put myself between them. I caught a fist on my left shoulder and before I could think it through I'd buried my right fist in his gut. He was tougher than he looked, too, and he didn't crumple. Instead, he got me pretty smartly on the chin, knocking me off the stool.

I'd never liked fighting, and I could feel the situation careening out of control. I barely heard the sound of the rest of the room breaking out into a brawl over the hammering of my heart. I scrambled under the table and got a chair in front of me like a shield. Black dots were appearing at the edges of my vision, and I knew I was panicking, but my expensive new reflexes knew what to do when a half-full mug whipped past my head and crashed into a nearby table, shards flying. I curled into a ball and tried to will myself to disappear as the sounds of a riot intruded into the safe space I was pretending to make for myself. I sat there for what seemed like hours before I remembered to lower my heart rate and moderate my endocrine system, and my brain started to work properly again.

I scanned the room for Grant and saw him huddling under a table with Bao. His eyes caught mine, and I jerked my head toward the door. He nodded, and I saw him talking to Bao. They shook their head, and it looked like he was trying to convince them of something, but it wasn't working. He looked my way, and I gave him the "now or never" hand signal. He nodded again and said something to Bao. They smiled sadly and shook their head again, and he blinked a few times. I got ready to run and wondered if he was going to come with me after all, then saw him give me a signal.

I thanked providence for allowing me to get some noodles into me, then sprang forward from behind my chair into a momentary break in the mêlée. Out of the corner of my eye I saw Grant scrambling along the floor toward the door that I was bounding toward. We made it through at about the same time and didn't bother talking as we ran down the hallway toward docking. We didn't stop until we were aboard Starlite Blue and had dogged the hatch behind us.

• • •

With both of us in the small cockpit there was barely enough room to turn around. "Now what?" Grant said, trying to find a patch of bulkhead to lean against comfortably.

"I don't know," I shrugged. "Find a way to get out of here, I guess."

"Then what?"

I looked at his face and wondered what we'd be losing by running. Wondered what we'd already lost. "Then either half the habitats in this sector blow each other out of the sky or they don't. Either someone comes to their senses and the Alliance and the Progressives start talking to each other, or they don't. And even if it all blows over, the mess going on in there isn't going to end overnight. We're a lot safer out there in the big black than we are here where all anyone cares about is the colour of your citizenship card."

"You really think so?" he said. "Where do you think you can go? The rustic climes of the outer colonies? No one there has any use for a couple of smugglers. And you," he pointedly raked his eyes over my body. "You really want to go live in exile in some place where there's nothing for you to do but be vilified? You're really willing to give up everything that makes you who you are just to be a little safer?"

"It doesn't matter who I am if I'm dead, Grant. There isn't going to be anything left for any of us here." I breathed deeply, forced my adrenaline levels back down. "Maybe we could start our own colony, those of us who leave. Or just keep moving, I don't know. But if we stay here, we're probably going to be killed. You saw the mess back in the hall. We both know that they're going to tear that place apart. And if you go back to Nune..." I couldn't finish the thought. I don't think I'd ever been so tired in my life.

Grant shook his head. "I'm not staying on Cyndex, but I'm not running, either, April. I don't like the way this is heading any more than you, but I'm a Progressive citizen. I'm willing to fight for what I believe, for the way I want to live my life. I can't see why, of all of us, you're not doing the same."

"This isn't like standing up to some ignorant neighbour," I said. "Sure, I love my freedom, but I love my life more. I'm going to do what I have to in order to survive. And I'd have thought you'd understand that."

"I do understand," he said, his voice suddenly quiet. "We all have to do what we have to do. If this blows over there's going to be a lot of rebuilding to do, a lot of materials to move. And if it doesn't blow over..." He looked at me, his eyes hard and clear. "If it doesn't blow over, running won't matter."

It didn't make sense—his eagerness to fight, to maybe even die, over the conflicts of people he'd never even met. Corporate leaders, politicians, generals. But I did know there wasn't anything I could say to change his mind. "At least let me help your ship get out. I have the override to the station's docking system."

Grant smiled, but there wasn't much of the warmth I'd always known from him. "Trading data has its perks."

I nodded. "Once you're on deck, I'll spring the clamps in five."

"Thanks," he said, and put a hand on my shoulder. "Maybe I'll see you somewhere down the line, buy you a beer."

"Sure," I said. I looked out the viewport at what used to be a nice quiet patch of space at the edge of nowhere. "It's quiet out there for now, better go."

"Take care of yourself, April."

"You, too, Admiral."

He undogged the hatch and stepped onto the station. "My name's Kwende," he said, then turned away. I could hear his feet pounding the metal floor as I swung the hatch closed.

I scanned my dashboard. Power levels were good, the lanes were clear, and I ignored the percussive thumps of weapons fire that made their muffled way from the station through the hull my little ship. I hit some keys on the dash and felt the docking clamps release.

"Good luck, Kwende Grant," I said to empty space as I swung my leg over the saddle and got ready to ride.

UNEXPECTEDLY TRANS-PARENT

Lydia Rogue

Kai adjusted their helmet one last time, uncharacteristically nervous before launch. Over the comms, mission control was calmly counting down.

On the display screen in front of them, a message from their wife, Venus, popped up. *Bring me back something?* They always tried to bring back some small memento for her, something that wouldn't make the customs office sigh at them, like a nice rock—non-radioactive, of course (they only made that mistake *once*).

They smiled and tapped out *Of course* just as the countdown reached zero and they began to pedal, bike zipping forward just as the rip in space/time opened up.

The portals were formally called "interstellar folds in the space-time continuum" but most cyclists and mission control just called it a Rip. They were the easiest way to get around the galaxy and visit all the planets, both human and alien—even if the Rips were a tad unpredictable at times.

That's where Kai and their coworkers came in. Sometimes they were hired by refugees fleeing a dead or dying planet to go back and find something—often a piece of technology or a rich person's heirloom—while other times a passing ship might pick up on something and report it back for investigation. That, with a side of courier work between currently inhabited planets, kept them plenty busy.

"Periwinkle Blue, this is Mission Control, latest readouts give you an hour and a half on the ground before the next Rip."

Sighing, they tapped their comms unit as they pedaled. It never felt like there was something beneath them when bicycling through the back end of space, but if they stopped pedaling they could get lost. "Understood. Any further insight as to what I'm looking for?"

"Negative. Survey ship turned over the data they had—looks like something organic?"

"Goddammit, am I tracking down another cat?"

That had been a bit of a nightmare of a ride—they looked like they'd lost a fight with a cactus for weeks after. Apparently cats and bicycles don't mix.

"Looks like it's bigger than that—possibly food?"

Kai grunted in acknowledgement as they phased out of the Rip and back onto solid ground. They tried not to leave large stores of food behind if they were still good when they were found—doubly so if Homeworld was expecting refugees to come in from the planet.

As the new world settled into view, they tried not to stare too much. So often the worlds they visited looked like home. In this case, it looked like they'd ridden into a 23rd century historical village. Sleek high-rise buildings towered over them as they pedaled down the empty streets.

Their geiger counter showed zero radiation, and their HUD readouts reported a breathable atmosphere, leaving them wondering why the inhabitants had left the world behind. Maybe they'd see them some day back on their homeworld.

Regardless, they were here with a job to do, and that was to fetch whatever had been left behind.

Kai let out a curse under their breath as they closed in on the coordinates and realized their target was moving. "Mission control, my target is moving. You didn't send me after the local wildlife did you?"

It took some time for the response to come back. "Periwinkle Blue, as far as we know there is no wildlife in the area big enough to show up on scans, but it is possible."

Everyone had heard of the cyclist who had the misfortune of being sent after an alligator—one that was very unhappy to see her.

They sighed and parked their bike alongside what appeared to be an apartment building. "Understood," they said.

The front door to the building opened easily—the remains of an electronic lock no longer functioning—and they made their way to the stairs, as their target seemed to be several stories above them.

When they exited the stairwell onto the correct floor, they paused, confused, as they heard what sounded like very faint music. Perhaps there was something here that still worked as expected—though if the electricity wasn't working any more, there shouldn't have been anything left that could make music.

Regardless, they followed the music as it was in the same direction as their target, just a quick jaunt down the hall.

There was a door half-open leading into one of the apartments. Kai strode in with confidence only to stutter to a halt when they spotted the source of the music—a *child*.

• • •

Later, in the mission report, they said that they reacted appropriately to the situation and declined to elaborate.

This meant they screamed.

So did the child.

"God what the *actual* fuck," they blurted out, only to realize they probably shouldn't curse in front of a child. Hopefully the translator wouldn't know what language to translate to.

"That's a bad word!"

No such luck.

They took a deep breath and agreed. "Sorry about that. You startled me." A child. An actual honest to god living breathing human being. As far as Kai knew, there had never been a case of a human being retrieved during one of these missions.

"Who are you?" the kid asked, hands on their hips. They were probably about 7 or 8, and they looked as confused as Kai felt.

"My name is Kai. What's yours?"

Their eyes narrowed. "Fitz."

"That's a cool name," Kai said. "How'd you end up here all by yourself?"

They shrugged. "I hid when everyone left. They didn't like me much and so I hid away even though they were looking really hard for me, then they never came back. Do you believe me when I say that's my name?"

"I think that's the name you want me to use and that's good enough for me," Kai said. They checked their readouts—about 45 minutes to get Fitz back to the Rip's location.

"How'd you get here?"

"I came by bike. I travel all around the galaxy to find things that people leave behind on dying planets." Crap, maybe they shouldn't have said that.

Fitz took a step back. "Did my parents send you?"

"Nope," they said. "Someone who was passing by spotted you and suggested we come make sure you were okay, maybe take you somewhere less lonely."

Fitz's lower lip trembled. "Are you sure my parents didn't send you?"

"Yeah kiddo," they said. "Come on, it'll be warm and I'll take you on a ride on my bike." They extended their hand and Fitz took it. "Grab anything you want that fits in a backpack—we can't come back."

A mad dash around the apartment later, and the two of them piled onto the bike. Fitz fit comfortably into the trailer, even if that wasn't what it was meant for.

"Mission control, target acquired. Set up a level 5 quarantine for my return trip."

The delay was even longer this time. "Periwinkle—level *five*? Are you sure?"

"Mission control, that's affirmative. I'll see you in ten minutes."

Level five was the highest rating of quarantine there was. Usually reserved for dangerous materials or, in this case, people. It ensured no diseases got out.

"Okay Fitz, hold on tight, this is going to get weird."

• • •

The other side of the Rip was a flurry of activity. Unlike when they had brought back the cat, their suit was unpunctured and so Kai was free to leave quarantine.

Fitz settled into the small room, waving at the cameras and pulling out some of the things the two of them had brought back with them.

Kai was immediately dragged into a mission debrief.

"A person," their manager said, staring down at the report in disbelief. "A *child*."

"Yup," Kai said, rubbing their face with their hand. "Do you think the ship knew?"

"I don't think so," Diego said, flipping through the initial mission brief. "Either way, once they're out of quarantine I don't even know what to do with them. Put them up for adoption, I guess? But that's going to be one hell of a paperwork nightmare."

"Do I win this month's prize for most unique find?" Kai asked, grinning. The last time they'd won the silly prize was when they'd found the cat. Apparently they had a knack for finding living things.

Diego laughed. "Yeah, we already got it printed up for you, even though there's three more days before the end of the month."

There were a couple more points of bureaucratic paperwork, as well as a review of their body camera, before they were released to head back home.

• • •

Kai let themself into their apartment quietly, smiling as they heard their wife muttering over the papers she was grading.

They took off their shoes and walked up behind her, wrapping their arms around her shoulders. "How were the kiddos?" they asked.

She groaned, leaning back. "I don't know why I gave them all a test today—two days after their essays were due. I should have listened when you said I'd regret having all that grading to do."

Kai planted a kiss on her forehead. "Maybe next year you'll remember."

"Maybe," she said, eyes drifting closed. "How was work? Did you bring me something?"

Occasionally they couldn't bring something back—the world was too dangerous or too far gone or it was too secretive of a mission.

This time they had just forgotten in the mess of finding Fitz.

Or had they? They looked past their partner and to the flyers she'd picked up a few days ago about adoption. Biological kids were an option for them, but neither of them wanted to pursue it—too much dysphoria all around. "Well...I have to talk to Diego, but..." they trailed off, not sure how to start this conversation.

Venus followed their gaze to the adoption information. "Kai...?"

They sat down next to her on the couch and explained Fitz, as best they could.

• • •

Four days later, Fitz was released from quarantine with a clean bill of health.

Two hours after that, Kai took them home in their bike.

ROVERS

Marcus Woodman

Outside the frame of what was once Oldfather Hall in Lincoln, Nebraska, Fetch loaded letters, packages, and supplies—gathered from hours of digging through abandoned homes and businesses. The correspondence—everything he carried was "correspondence"—stacked high in his cart, and he considered expanding the carriage, but the bigger size made his bike too cumbersome around winding roads or uphill tracks. He tied everything down, instead.

The people in this Community were friendly enough, he supposed. With the time his rounds took, someone might be dead the next time he returned. The only people he saw more often than twice a year were other couriers—too busy, too rushed to stop and chat.

He uncapped his canteen and one of the residents poured carbon-filtered water into it. Her name was Liz, he was pretty sure.

"Thanks," Fetch said. Liz nodded and set the big pitcher down. "So, did you get the stuff I asked about last time? The testosterone?" He spoke in a quiet voice once he saw her expression shift from neutral to tense.

"Trust me, Fetch, I advocated as much as I could for you," she said. He deflated and she patted his shoulder with a tight smile. She always seemed so uncomfortable with him. "I know it's hard, but medicine's tough. Any factories these days are geared for, well, life-saving drugs." He shook her hand away.

"Right. Sure. See you." Never mind. Before the wells ran dry, before the mines all collapsed, they hadn't quite gotten to trans folks' needs yet. The many still voted on the needs of the few today.

Fetch went back to his bike, where a couple of kids pointed at the solar panel on its motor. He shooed them away, saw their sad faces, and decided to talk to them to sate his guilt.

"How fast does it go all charged up?" one kid said.

"Twenty miles per hour or so," Fetch said.

"Why don't you have a partner like the other couriers?" the other kid said. Fetch remembered the peculiar looks he got from people whenever he visited Communities, or even bumped into other couriers. Remembered that feeling of walking just beside his body, never aligning with it. It hurt—all of it.

"I just like the solitude," he said. He strapped on his gear—leather pants, boots, jacket, elbow and knee pads, gloves, helmet. A survival dagger at his belt. Legally, it was supposed to be strapped sideways across his back. But these days, the government had no presence. Suits never bothered him.

Fetch kicked up the stand on his bike, hit the motor's switch, and sped off. It puttered away towards Des Moines with a hum and a shake.

"Stay safe!" Liz called after him. He ignored her.

• • •

Fetch knew the road well. He knew all the fastest routes. Maybe he flirted with danger a little too much, but some days, he didn't mind the idea of running into raiders or even into some lunging, crazed mutant. He wondered if the suits ever investigated those shiny-eyed creatures out there. They looked almost human sometimes, so rumors and legends spread.

In Communities without web access—like the ones he mostly served—people said the creatures were nuclear victims' shades. Others claimed they were mangy coyotes, or wolves that traveled southeast from Yellowstone and got "weird." They were too big, though. Fetch only saw them once, and they were far off. Sure, they creeped him out, but he was more concerned with raiders or self-servers.

Night dropped like a big, black feather. The sky out here was so large, anyone could see the moon and stars creep forward for their turn to light the planet's pyre. Bugs wailed for mates and their cries crossed the empty fields. Fetch sensed his motor slowing and switched to analog power—his own legs—'til he found a bridge crossing Highway 2. It'd do for a night.

"Hey, there." A voice jolted Fetch from his thoughts as he tossed down his sleeper. In one hand he grasped his dagger, in the other he held his flashlight and shone it in the intruder's face. The stranger—a man, hairy, a few inches taller than him but not by much—held his hand over his squinting eyes and stepped back. All 'round his fingers were silver rings, thick and thin, and dangling from his neck was an oval pendant, also silver. They flashed in the spotlight.

"I'm a courier—all I've got is correspondence that isn't rightly mine or yours," Fetch said. "Back off."

"I know you're a courier, and I don't want any of that," the man said with his eyes to the ground. "I'm no raider—just in need of some help, alright? See, look." He pulled up the leg of his pants to reveal a blood-soaked, seeping bandage on his shin. Fetch lowered the spotlight to the stranger's leg and winced.

"What's your name?" he said.

"Den," he said. "Short for Aiden." Fetch snorted.

"How old are you? In your sixties?" he said. The old-timer—though he *looked* like he was thirty-something—chuckled.

"Hey, watch it," he said. "When I was your age, it was one of the hottest baby names in America."

Fetch squinted. He had no idea when that was. But nonetheless, this was no raider. Most likely.

"Why're you out here alone?" Fetch said. "You an individualist?"

"Hell no." Den grimaced and shook his head. "My folks got scattered by raiders a few days back. Been hiding out since then. So, can I hitch a ride, or what?"

Fetch looked between Den and his cart. If he expanded it, he'd fit on it alright.

"How much do you weigh?" he said.

"C'mon. You've barely got any weight on there. I just want to get to the next Community." Fetch thought it over before nodding.

"All right. But I'm warning you—no weird shit." Den nodded and lowered his hands.

"Thanks," he said. "Here—I got something good that I'll trade for your help." He hobbled back to the other side of the highway, then returned with a big, green bolster. Den tossed it to the ground and yanked a cord. The fabric billowed out with a zipping noise, jostled, and popped out to become a tent. Fetch raised his eyebrows.

"That big enough for both of us?" he said.

"Yeah—you just use it, though. I'll be alright out here," Den said and smiled.

"That's dumb. You're injured, not me."

"I'd rather respect your privacy." Den stumbled over to the wall under the bridge, where one of its ends met a hill. "Well, good night." He tossed down a blanket and plopped onto it. Fetch stared at him with a sour expression. He rolled up his bedroll and tumbled it to Den.

"Use this, at least," Fetch said.

"You're the one doing *me* a favor," Den said.

"So what?" Fetch ducked into the tent. "People should help each other these days." He zipped up the flap.

"Guess you're right." Den unfurled the bedroll and settled in.

The bugs settled down, too, and shut up for the night.

• • •

The road was long and Fetch did not look forward to spending it with company. Especially after learning what Den's sense of humor was like.

"So what's your name, anyway?" Den had asked before they set off.

"Fetch." Den laughed—cracked up, actually. Fetch glared.

"A courier named Fetch? Really?" Den said through chuckles.

"Yeah, just keep that up," Fetch said with a sigh as he started up his bike's motor. Den quieted down.

"Sorry—you aren't gonna leave me, right?" he said.

"A promise is a promise," Fetch said and sighed again, louder.

"Thanks. You've probably been teased enough." Den rubbed the back of his head sheepishly as he got aboard the carriage. Fetch said nothing. Nobody usually commented on his name, which was more of a nickname, anyway. Truth was, he never thought that hard about what new name he wanted, back when he decided his old one no longer suited him. When someone asked what his name was, he just thought "Fetch" sounded funny. It stuck.

"I guess I prodded you for being named Aiden, so we're even," Fetch said. "How's your ankle? You think it'll need antibiotics?" Den shook his head. He lifted his pant leg to show it off.

"Like I said, just resting and not working it too hard made it much better," he said. Fetch squinted at it. Like Den promised, the injury looked smaller, less fetid. Like a clean cut.

"...You heal way fast," he said. "You've had that for how long, again?"

"A couple days, but like I said, I've been walking. You should've seen it when I first got it—it looked like the bone was peeking out!" Den laughed; Fetch stayed silent. He shifted gears and his bike lurched forward.

"Sounds like it was real bad," he said and swallowed. He needed to change the topic. "Say, what's that pendant?"

"Surprised you noticed," Den said. He unstrung it from his neck and passed it over.

The pendant looked very old, and the carving on its front was shallow and worn from years of touch. Fetch could make out a simple image of a man with a dog's head. The figure serenely carried a cross in one arm and looked up to the sky. Fetch handed it back.

"Who's that?" he said.

"Saint Christopher," Den said. "Though on most icons of him, he's just big and bearded, not beastly."

"You religious?" Fetch said.

"Nah. I just like the story."

"What's the story?" Den stretched out and scratched his stomach.

"Long story short, Christopher—he had a different name, before—was from a race of monstrous, dog-headed men. He wanted to serve the most powerful king he could find, so he went out and searched for him," he said while he strung it 'round his neck again. "On his journey, he learned of the Devil, and he thought that Satan was the most powerful king. So, that's who he wanted to serve. He was terribly fearsome—a true monster.

"But then he learned that there was someone even more powerful than the Devil out there—Christ. He wanted to serve Christ, instead, but didn't know what to do. Eventually, he started helping folks cross this deep river. One day, this kid comes up to him, and Christopher carries the kid on his shoulders. But the kid starts getting heavier and heavier, and his feet start sinking into the mud along the bottom.

"He keeps going, even though he nearly drowns, even if he could've dropped the kid and saved his own hide. When they get to the other side, turns out that the kid is Christ. Christ commended him for bearing the weight of the world on his shoulders, and gave him a new name, which means 'Christ-bearer.'"

Fetch peered over his shoulder with a raised brow.

"That's a pretty spiritual story. So if you aren't religious, why wear it?" he said. Den laughed.

"Not religious doesn't mean the same as not superstitious," he said. "This guy protects folks moving from one space to the next. I do that a lot, even when I'm staying put." Fetch cocked his head, but let it go. They traveled for a long time in near-silence after that, with only vague, meaningless comments.

"We're gonna reach a good resting stop," Fetch said as the sun dipped down. "Want to call it a night?"

Den nodded and examined his leg. The wound was just about cleared up. "Sounds good," he said. "Gotta eat something, anyway."

Fetch stared at his leg, but said nothing.

They pulled into the rest stop and build their camp inside. Old rest stops stood up damn well, in part thanks to Couriers knowing that fellow travelers used them as refuge from hyperstorms—they started as category five hurricanes becoming the norm, blizzards in mid-March, 100-year floods *every* year, and only got worse, faster than any politician could prepare for. Around here, hyperstorms showed up as tornadoes wider than a mile. The funnels ripped buildings to pieces and twisted the trunks of stubborn trees. The rest stops were updated so their foundations and structures survived storms like this, but they needed a bit of TLC sometimes. Fetch got to work patching up the wooden planks covering the glass doors. It was only polite to do what he could to make it easier on the next traveler. Den chipped in, too, by climbing onto the roof and covering holes. He grew on Fetch a little, for that.

"You don't worry, stopping in a place like this?" Den said while they supped on preserved soup and jam. Fetch shrugged.

"Everyone needs shelter from hyperstorms sometimes," he said. "Tacit law, I guess. I've shared a rest stop with self-servers and even raiders before. We ate, slept, and moved on once the storm cleared." Den nodded with a hum of intrigue.

"We've all got some shared responsibility for each other, these days," he said. Fetch nodded back.

They finished up their meals and turned in to sleep. In the darkness, water dripped from an old pipe, still barely functioning after all these years. Just moments after their breathing slowed, the pipe creaked under the weight of a clawed foot. The dripping's pace picked up, a frantic heartbeat yet to spread. Padded steps crept closer to Den and Fetch when their eyes opened.

Fetch, inside Den's pop-up tent, saw only shadows. Huge, wolflike. Thick, shaggy chests sprouted lanky limbs, strong necks, pinned ears, bared teeth. Yellow, gleaming eyes. Three of the figures surrounded them. Fetch's breath stuck in his throat and his heart caught up to the drips.

"Great to see you all again!" Den said. "Maybe you'll sit put and quit the antics this time." He shivered as he spoke. Fetch stayed silent—absolutely silent. The creatures snarled and spat and barked. With trembling hands, Fetch reached for the knife at his side.

Before he could grab its hilt, Den lurched and his back expanded in size. His hands cracked as they lengthened into claws. His shirt tore. Fur burst from its shreds. His ears pointed, his jaw extended, and pearly fangs sprouted from his gums. The silver necklace and rings caught the light, glinting.

The other three rushed him. In a tangle of teeth and fur and claws, Fetch lost sight of Den. He dropped to his knees, pushed himself into the corner of the tent, and sobbed. He was going to die, and the correspondence would go undelivered.

The part of him that hated what the world became wondered if it would actually be so bad.

The barking and snarling attacked his covered ears. Things fell and broke and clattered and scattered. After several long, long minutes, the roars gave way to whines and yips. Three of the beasts ran, one remained.

His form—was it Den, or another?—shuddered with each ragged breath. Hot puffs blew from his open maw as he panted. He let out a sound between a wail and a moan and shrunk down. From his fingers, one of the rings dropped to the ground.

"Shit," he said. It was Den. "Shit. Missed again." He turned and hesitated before the tent. "Fetch? You OK in there?"

"Get away!" Fetch yelled, voice cracking. "I'll—I'll stab you if you get close, monster!" Den held up his hands.

"Woah!" he said. "I'm in control, see? You've got nothing to fear—*ha ha*." That forced chuckle sent blood racing to Fetch's head.

"Nothing to fear?" he repeated. "Nothing?!"

"Yeah. I won't hurt you."

"You brought them here! You're working with them!"

"Fetch, if I'd been working with them, you'd be long dead."

Den spoke so clearly, so deadpan—so unlike his usual, sing-song tone-that he convinced Fetch on the spot. Fetch lowered his knife.

"All right," he said, shaken. "You've got a point."

"Are you gonna come out?" Den said after a moment of waiting. "I could use a little help." Fetch took a breath, let it out, and opened the flap. Den was covered in bloodied shreds and scratches, his shirt torn to bits. Underneath the gouges and the mess, Fetch noticed two distinct, ragged lines beneath Den's pectorals. They cut from under his arms and met in the center, only a few inches apart from each other.

Fetch's eyelids fluttered. He recognized their meaning instantly—they etched history into Den's body.

Den smiled through his wounds.

"I got nicked pretty bad," he said. "I just want some help cleaning up."

"S-sure." Fetch climbed out of the tent. He looked around the rest stop and saw just how destructive the fight had been. Storage cases were knocked to their sides. One of the wooden barriers on the doors laid in two broken halves. Blood and fur littered the floor. An errant fang was stuck in an old display case with a model of Iowa inside.

Worst of all, his bike and carriage and everything in it lied scattered on the ground. Its motor and solar convertor were destroyed. Fetch clutched his hair.

"Oh, no."

"I'm sorry," Den said. "I threw one of them into it and—"

"Forget it. Whatever. We'll get to it later," Fetch said. Den slumped, pathetic as the beaten dog he was.

They sat in silence as Fetch cleaned clotted blood from Den's wounds, using his medikit's sparse contents. As he wiped blood away, he swore he saw Den's wounds shrinking. He could ignore it no longer. The question burned.

"What *are* you?"

"You really don't know?" Den said with a raised brow. "Guess ever since the floods and the heatwaves, villains from fairytales stopped being so scary. I'm a werewolf—a person who changes into a wolf."

"Is that what those other creatures are, then?" Fetch said. Den nodded. "Why were they trying to kill us?"

"They can't help it—they're just hungry."

"Just—?!" Fetch's eyes widened.

"I used to be like that, too, but look—I can control it now." As Den spoke, his voice turned into a growl, his ears pointed, his nose grew into a muzzle—

"Stop. I get it," Fetch said and looked away.

"They need to be subdued, not killed. I just need to give them these," Den said. From his belt pouch, he removed a handful of silver jewelry—rings, necklaces, earrings, piercings, and a couple more pendants of Saint Christopher. They still had price tags on them, likely scavenged from a ruined jewelry store. "Silver calms the beast. I don't know how, or why, but trust me—it's worked for all the others, too." Fetch kept bandaging him. As he dabbed a cut on Den's chest, he bit his lip. Those scars called to his deepest needs.

"One more question," he said.

"Shoot."

"Are you trans?"

"Yep."

"How are you so—so masculine?" Fetch caught himself. "I'm trans too. But T's in short supply. *No* supply."

"I know—about the T and about you," Den said.

"How'd you know?" Fetch wondered what gave it away. Den chuckled and shook his head.

"You stick out your jaw to make it look squarer," he said. "I did the same thing before this grew in." He rubbed his beard. Fetch forced himself to relax. His jaw pulled back into its proper place. "Anyway, all this hair's not from T. Testosterone never gave me this much, even after years of using it. I got it after I turned."

"Into a werewolf?"

"Yup."

A wild idea flashed through Fetch's head. But he shelved it.

"We've gotta figure out the bike," he said. "I still need to make deliveries."

"Right." Den nodded. They got to work. They rigged its chain back in place and unbent the wheels as best as they could. The repairs would have to do until they found proper replacement parts—but the solar panel for the motor was a total loss.

"Well, so much for that," Fetch said and tossed his wrench back into its toolbox. It clanged against everything else. Den sucked his lips around his teeth and sighed through his nose.

"How far are we from the next Community?" he said. Fetch hung his head and shook it.

"I should've been able to reach Des Moines in a week from today, but now it'll take more than two, if I have no motor," he said. "I can only keep pedaling for so long."

"Do you *have* to pedal?" Den said.

"Of course. How else will it go?" Den stood and patted dust and mud from his pants.

"Got a chain? I'll pull you," he said. Fetch stared at him.

"You just got mauled by werewolves."

"They're shallow wounds, not like what I got earlier."

"You're insane."

"I'm strong." Den grinned as his hair grew shaggier and his ears pointed.

"It's daylight! If another traveler sees you—!"

"So call me an irradiated pooch from Cooper Nuclear." Den laughed at his own joke. His chuckles sounded more like barks, once he transformed completely.

They had no other options. Fetch hooked a chain to his bicycle and Den wrapped it around his powerful torso. They walked the bike back out onto the highway. Den lurched forward, slowly, arduously—and picked up pace.

He ran down on all fours along the hot, broken, asphalt highway. He panted out of excitement, more than fatigue. The wind whipped through his fur and cooled him.

Fetch whooped and hung tight to the handlebars, keeping his front tire as straight as he could. The chain grunted around the gears and the spokes clicked against the frame, but it *worked*. They'd be in Des Moines right on time, at this rate.

When Den tired, Fetch took over pedaling with him on the back. But he recuperated fast, and seemed eager to get back to running. After a few more nights of frantic travel, they saw the glint of the golden dome of the old Iowan capitol building.

The moment they passed the Des Moines city limit sign, Den and Fetch stopped at the side of the road, hugged each other, and collapsed, an exhausted heap.

"We're here," Fetch said, grinning. "We made it!" Den nodded and grinned back.

"Let's find civilization, yeah?" he said. His stomach growled, they laughed, and they moved on.

• • •

Eventually, they came to the Des Moines Community. Fetch passed the mail to its various organizers with mumbled apologies for the damage on some packages and letters. He and Den settled down for a few nights, eating like kings and celebrating their success while Fetch's bike got repaired.

But the mail still needed to be delivered, and Fetch and Den needed to leave. Den packed up his things one night, and Fetch approached him in the old house they were staying in.

"Are you going already?" Fetch said. Den nodded.

"I've gotta keep hunting those packs," he said. "They move quick, and they'll be here sooner than later. I can't risk them attacking a Community." Fetch frowned and tightened his lips.

"Before you go, I wanted to ask something of you," he said. Den turned and faced him. "Would you travel with me, and would you turn me, too?" Den's eyes widened. He looked over Fetch's face before frowning.

"You know, it isn't just muscles and hair," he said. "You get hunger pains bad. You stink like wet dog when it's hot. And the wanderlust—it's awful."

"I'm a courier. Wanderlust is my job," Fetch said.

"The others will sniff you out no matter where you go. They'll always be drawn to your scent."

"Den, please." Fetch's throat tightened. "If you come with me, we'll be able to watch out for each other. And if you don't, I'll figure it out. But I can't live with *this* anymore." He gestured at his body with drooping shoulders. Den hesitated. He closed his eyes and sighed. Then he looked straight at Fetch and pointed at him.

"You can't take the silver off, ever," he said. Fetch brightened up and a smile curled his lips.

"I won't," he said.

"If your jewelry falls off, every time the moon gets near-full, you'll get lost, and you might not wake up to yourself again 'til I catch your sorry ass."

"I'll be careful."

"You might die if you lose it. You might kill someone, without even realizing it."

Fetch hesitated, but he fisted his hands and met Den's gaze.

"Then I'll cut myself open and sew one of your pendants up inside," he said. Den watched his face. He allowed himself to smile.

"Attaboy," he said and took one of the pendants from his pouch. He handed it over. "Put it on." Fetch strung it 'round his neck and tightened the slipknots in the back until it hung just under his collarbone. "Are you ready? You'll shift for the first time after I bite you. It's intense. But the silver will keep you keen."

"I'm ready," Fetch said. Den changed into his wolf self once more. As he grew in size and shape, Fetch's heart beat faster. Soon, Den towered over him and looked down at him through gleaming eyes.

"It will hurt," he said. His words came out distorted and choppy; the muzzle made it difficult to form words, and the timbre of his voice changed. "Blood must break for it to spread."

"I understand."

"Where shall I bite you?" Fetch tilted his head and tugged the shoulder of his shirt off.

"Here." He pointed to the nape of his neck. Den wrapped his arms around Fetch and clasped him tight. He sank his teeth into Fetch's shoulder, quickly as he could; too slow, and it would hurt too much. Fetch bit back his yelp and stiffened. Once Den tasted iron in his maw, he released Fetch and let him go limp in his arms. Fetch's eyelids fluttered and his pulse quickened. As blood spread through his whole body, he trembled and blushed.

It was a peculiar sensation, growing hair so quickly. Sort of itchy, sort of tickly. He expected his face to hurt when his muzzle grew, but his jaw mostly felt tight. Bones and joints cracked and lengthened, rearranged to fit his new physique. Muscles swelled with new strength. The tail was the oddest feeling of all, like a sudden, powerful ripple down his spine.

A tremor shook his entire body from the bottom up. He jolted, craned his neck, and a howl burst from his lips.

• • •

Fetch collapsed to the floor, human-shaped once again, after only a few moments of being a werewolf. Den watched over him until he awoke. When he saw Fetch's eyes flutter open, he smiled down at him.

"How're you feeling?" he said.

"Tired." Fetch sat up and scratched his face. His eyes widened—the beginnings of a beard sprouted from his chin. Den laughed.

"Fast, isn't it?" he said. "Take it easy for a few days. Don't transform—you'll get too tired, otherwise." Fetch nodded, and Den got serious once again. "And remember, we're pack animals—when they catch your scent, they'll come after you, no matter how lost they are. They'll seek you, for good or bad."

"I'll be ready," Fetch said and weakly waved his hand.

"Will you?" Den cocked his head. "You're new to this. You're a pup."

"Yeah." Fetch turned his head and looked up at him. "You're coming with me, right?" Den watched his face, then turned back to the ground before him. His heart thumped—Fetch could hear it.

"Yeah," Den said. "I could."

"So do."

"But—"

"How long have you been alone?"

Den paused. Thought.

"Pretty long." He sighed. "Really long."

"You said it yourself." Fetch smiled and watched the sky past the holes in the ceiling, eyes still sleepy and lidded. "We're pack animals."

"You'd want me around, even if it's dangerous?" Den looked down at him with big, forlorn eyes. Fetch laughed.

"My job's already dangerous. I've needed a partner for a while, now." He met Den's eyes again. "So, how about it?"

• • •

Back in Lincoln, after six months of traveling around the Midwest, Fetch and Den arrived at the Community with deliveries and dogs in tow. Though, these two dogs looked human, right now. Fetch introduced them to Liz—she looked both bewildered and happy to see Fetch—and got them set up as official members of Oldfather Community.

“Is that really you, Fetch?” Liz said once the werewolves wandered off. Fetch scratched his carefully-cultivated beard with a smile.

“Yeah,” he said.

“So, did some other Community get what you needed?”

Fetch looked over at Den while he briefed the werewolves on their silver embellishments. One pierced a hoop through her septum, the other wore a chain ‘round his neck. He noticed Fetch watching and waved at him with a grin.

“You could say that,” Fetch said without taking his eyes off Den.

Liz set him up with the correspondence for the next trip. As he walked through the Community with Den, he was met with curious stares and uncertain smiles. The kids who always seemed fascinated with his bike seemed more interested in his new look, this time. Den rested his hand on Fetch’s shoulders.

“Should we rest up?” he said. Fetch thought it over while he pushed his bike along. He stared off into the long, empty road before them, the cool blue, cloudless sky like a dome over their heads. He looked back at his carriage, full of letters with research notes, news, heartfelt notes, gifts, and valuable supplies.

“Nah,” he said. “We’ve got delivers to make and dogs to catch.” Den chuckled and patted his back.

And they left, back to their duty, back to their pack.

THE VISITMOTHERS

Charlie Jane Anders

Cait walks her creaky old five-speed bicycle up the fumbly narrow path on the steep grade of Toothache Hill. At the top she says the nonsense words you're supposed to say, somewhere between a prayer and a petition and an invocation, that will make the Visitmothers show up. Nothing happens. (Except the wind gets stronger and colder, and two middle-aged people give up on foraging for stray Pokémon and trudge down into the curvy crinkly streets of the city.) Cait hugs herself and fidgets, and says the whole thing again, trying not to shiver or bite into the words.

The sun goes down. Cait fumbles in the old knapsack bungee-corded to the back of the bicycle for her hoodie, which is fuzzy on the inside and almost reaches bathrobe levels of comfort despite being so old that the logo on the breast is illegible. A smattering of stars shows through the city light pollution, and yet the moon glows so bright it almost throbs, with its surface visible in crisp detail.

The bike wobbles in the wind, so Cait leans it more carefully against a rock. This Raleigh Chopper has been Cait's constant accompaniment, ever since her sixteenth birthday, and she's used to seeing the world from atop its seat. She has decorated its spokes with rainbow colors, streamers come out of its handlebars, and the seat is covered with a leopard-print fabric.

Cait is going to have a scary ride home on these streets. City darkness, but still...darkness. She should leave right now, but she's come all this way, memorized the words, psyched herself up. She doesn't want to go home with nothing. Not because of her iron willpower or determination or whatever, but because she cannot imagine what she will do if this doesn't work. She doesn't have any back-up plan.

So she sits on the crest of Toothache Hill, checking the time on her phone constantly until she risks draining the battery. She sings the entire Purple Rain album to herself from memory. The shouts of drunk people fill the streets, then die down. The wind gets colder.

Finally, somewhere between one and two in the morning, a darkness gathers at the top of Toothache Hill. Not the dark of night, but more like a blindfold made of velvet. Cait's heart amps up. The Visitmothers have arrived at last.

It's just like everybody says in the stories Cait has heard late at night after too many drinks at the Too Queer Karaoke Night, or in certain message-board chats. Four Visitmothers descend from the sky but also seem to glide sideways, as if they were on a conveyor belt coming from someplace off to the side of the hill. They each flex five wings (or perhaps they're legs, or beaks, or something else) from their slender concave bodies, and sometimes the folds and creases on their bodies appear like faces. Pareidolia, probably.

You brought us to visit you, says the Visitmother closest to Cait. You want us to visit change upon you, to answer a question, or to predict. Those are the three visitations that humans desire. Which?

The Visitmothers have been appearing for a couple years now, and they've taught a few people the words that would invite them to high-up, isolated places. They only answer the occasional invitation, and you have to be very careful what you ask them—or, what you ask them for. They're fairies. Or aliens. Or alien fairies. Nobody really knows. But they know secrets, and their predictions come true. And if you go with them, they will change you according to your desires. But you have ask with precision, because they sometimes misunderstand the speech of humans.

Cait hesitates. Now that it's real, she can't even make a sound. Then she gathers her breath and blurts out words that she didn't practice nearly as much as that invocation. "I want to be changed. I feel so alone. I can't afford facial feminization surgery or any of the other things I need, and I never have anybody around who sees me for my true self. I want to be reshaped. Transformed. Give me wings and lasers. Give me extra knowledge, or understanding, or cleverness. Make me so beautiful that people have to catch their breath."

Then Cait just shakes her head, and speaks from her heart. "The real truth is, I just don't want to be alone anymore. That's all I really want. Everything else is just...just a means to an end." Speaking the truth feels too heavy to brace against, but a moment later, she feels light and kind of empty. And cold, again.

The Visitmothers seem to discuss among themselves for a moment. As you ask, it shall be done, the one in front says. Wings/legs/beaks flexing and bobbing.

And then...the Visitmothers gently take hold of Cait's wobbly old Raleigh five-speed, and pull it inside their black velvet interspace. The knapsack tumbles onto the rocky grass.

A moment later, the Visitmothers and Cait's bicycle are gone.

Cait is left alone on the top of Toothache Hill, cursing herself and the Visitmothers. Mostly herself, though. She worked so hard, she prepared, she coached herself, she studied other people's accounts of their own visits, and...she screwed up. They didn't understand. She spoke from her heart, she's sure about that, but not clear enough. She had one chance to make everything different. And now, she's as alone as she ever was—except that now, she's lost the one thing that always kept her company.

Long walk home. Cold gross streets, sloping upward and downward. Cait starts to wheeze, which gets in the way of blaming herself in a trudgy undertone.

When Cait gets home, she can't sleep for crying. At least tomorrow is Sunday, so she doesn't have to go to work. She sits on her futon and hugs herself and keeps pouring hot water on the same orange spice teabag over and over, until it just tastes like slightly bitter hot water. She glances at the mirror and remembers the three people who told her she was beautiful in the past month: Luke, Clarissa, Boz. She wishes she could believe them.

She wishes she didn't feel so alone.

Cait finally sets down the lukewarm mug and falls asleep. Her dreams suck, but she doesn't remember them.

She's awoken by a tapping on her apartment door—not like a person knocking, but like a backbeat, pounding over and over at slightly syncopated intervals. She goes to the door and doesn't see anything through the fish-eye. She's about to go back to bed, but the tapping keeps going.

At last, Cait, opens her door. And...it's her bike. Sort of.

Her bike has wings. And lasers. And it's so beautiful, she can't even breathe for a moment. And then once she can breathe, she can't see, because tears are stinging her eyes. She tries to speak, and can't.

Her bicycle speaks, instead. "Hey, I'm back," it says. "I'm still the same bicycle that carried you everywhere, your whole adult life. Except now, I can fly. Oh, and I understand the deep workings of the world. Thank you for doing this for me. I have all these thoughts going through my head, it's amazing. Yesterday I didn't even have any thoughts at all, or a head for that matter. There's so much I want to tell you about, but it'll take the rest of our lives to explain all of it. For now, I just want to feel your strong legs moving my pedals again."

So Cait climbs on her bike, still pouring tears, and the two of them race down the stairs of her apartment building, half rolling and half flying. Once they get outside, the bike flaps its wings—she's going to have to find out what pronoun the bike prefers—and they take to the air.

A moment later, they're soaring over the rooftops, as the city wakes up underneath them. They race away from the city, over the river and the mountains and the irregular polygons of farmland. The whole time, Cait's bicycle is whispering to her: things from her childhood that never made sense to her before, the hiding places of love letters people wrote a hundred years ago.

"You need a name," Cait says. "What do you want to be called?"

"I'm so new. I've only had words for a short time. Can you choose a name for now? I can always change it later."

Cait thinks for a moment, and then decides her bicycle will be called Brave.

"The most important thing you need to remember always," says Brave, "is that I can see you for your true self, and I'll always remind you. And I promise you'll never be alone again."

They fly so far and so fast that the sun keeps rising, over and over.

A SUDDEN DISPLACEMENT OF MATTER

Ava Kelly

The bar was rowdy for an early afternoon, the chatter ebbing and rising like the flow of tides with the updates coming in. Katja took another swig of her drink, eyes drawn to the holosphere hovering right beneath the ceiling. Dankmar was in outrage, and the newscasters seemed to compete on who could relay the most melodrama.

The Gender Equality Monument had been stolen, right from under the noses of an entire guard squad, but in Katja's opinion that didn't merit such a scandalized response. Dankmar, as the capital of the Free Station Coalition, was expected to be the place to display the symbols of the hard-earned autonomy each of the sixteen space stations had fought for. But Dankmar and its political class forgot that some of those symbols had been acquired in...unsavory ways. The statue of Seraphine Mardum, the first trans woman to become admiral, used to sit on Astara station, overlooking its ceremony hall. Katja knew for a fact that Astara's consul at the time had been tricked into handing it over. She shook her head. The GEM had been appropriated just the same, to sit in the square at the center of the station, in a neat row along with the symbols of all the other members, but a few steps behind the monument of Dankmar itself. It all smelled of Dankmar asserting dominance. Katja wrinkled her nose.

On the holosphere, the footage of the empty pedestal where the GEM used to sit ran in vivid color. Katja's distaste turned into amusement. Ehrentraud, the station represented by the GEM, had the unfortunate reputation of being the most mellow in the Coalition. Ehrentraud had started out as an enby shelter, a place where genderqueer people were the majority, but as they had fought for their independence from Earth, they had become the beacon of gender equality. From the outside, though, their demeanor of easy acceptance could be seen as a sign of weakness.

The image of an agitated announcer with blue eyebrows and green lipstick filled the screen. "This just in: the High Council has put out a bounty on the GEM and its thief. One—" They looked to the side, whispering, "Is this right?" before staring back into the camera. "One thousand units of credit and free water for life."

The momentary silence in the bar was overcome with hollers, hoots, and plans of action. The ruckus dimmed again when the official guard report was released. Most of it was political babble, but Katja listened closely nonetheless, and two pieces of information emerged. First, the monument had simply disappeared into thin air, leaving behind nothing but the faint smell of burned rubber. Second, guard officials had already interviewed the owner of the only docked ship flying the Ehrentraud flag and had determined they had played no part in the heist.

Perhaps that reputation wasn't so unfortunate after all. Some people might find it useful to hide behind an appearance of meekness, and although it wasn't Katja's style, she toasted the air in honor of the thief brave enough to best Dankmar's guard.

"I'm telling you," someone with a scratchy voice said somewhere behind Katja. "There's no way it was the 'traudian. I passed by the docks yesterday and saw them putting up a farald sign. The poor bastard is charging ten units a ride on a ship that looks like it's about to fall apart. Not very smart if you ask me. I wouldn't pay half a unit to go to Godra and back in that."

Katja shook her head. Falling into stereotyping and judgments was easy. Uprooting misconceptions, on the other hand, was much more difficult, but perhaps that had been the pilot's intent. Nobody in their right mind would ask for such a steep price, not when faralds were a micro-unit a dozen, transporting people in between stations on demand, zooming about in an abundance that made them the cheapest form of travel. Most of them asked for amounts that covered fuel, with little on top for profit, and it was all highly dependent on the state of their ship. She scratched at her cheek. The Ehrentraudian was either new to the faralding business, and thus unaware of its unspoken machinations, or they had ulterior, devious motives which Katja couldn't guess. Perhaps it was time she bought a ride.

• • •

Although she kept a low profile, Katja wasn't one of the best bounty hunters in the Coalition for nothing. On the way to the docks, she stopped by the central square to see if she could gauge anything that had been missed in the news. It was the sensible thing to do. During her life, she had tried and failed at many jobs, one of which had been an attempt to enlist in the guard. That particular endeavor had taught her how to mingle with them and how to subtly ask for information, especially the classified kind. Those skills helped her learn that nothing but the GEM had been taken, that even the metal hooks holding it in place hadn't been touched. And those were welded shut.

It was peculiar to say the least.

Just as she was about to head off, a hologram of the GEM flickered to life on top of the barren pedestal. The monument was made of an old bicycle. It was plain at a glance, didn't even have a propeller, only foot-activated pedals that required a being with legs to operate it. The metal bars forming its body were painted in stripes of yellow-white-purple-black, shining faintly. A closer look, however, revealed a series of more modern bikes painted around the saddle, bikes that were designed for riders with various disabilities. Katja's mom used to have one of those and she loved to wax poetic about all the ways the GEM wasn't just about gender. She wasn't wrong, but it wasn't relevant to the current situation, so Katja shook the memory away, turning her attention back to the present.

Up on the monitors adorning the facade of the council structure, an announcement ran explaining how the hologram was meant to avoid upsetting the people of Dankmar any further. Katja grimaced. If they could use such displays, why not do it permanently and give the stations their monuments back?

The sudden disdain she felt was so strong that she reconsidered going after the GEM's thief. But even without the desire to collect on the bounty, she was too curious to pass on the opportunity to figure out what exactly had happened, who this bold thief was, and most importantly how they did it.

With that in mind, she ducked into her rented bunk to grab her stuff and change her clothes. As utilitarian as her hunter uniform was, it wasn't the best option, not if she wanted to gain the Ehrentraudian pilot's trust. Her favorite disguise was a medic persona, and it helped that she had had to patch herself up in the past. She could do a fairly good impression and even offer basic medical assistance in a pinch.

• • •

The ship, bearing the generic designation ARN 5064 instead of a custom name, looked...decrepit was a nice way of putting it. Katja wondered for a moment how it was even held together under all the rust and flaking solar panels. Out front, next to the ramp leading up to the airlock, there was a sign proclaiming Farald, 10, any destination. Highly irregular, since faralds usually had preferences about where they traveled. It had to be a cover to get out of Dankmar without raising suspicion.

Katja ran up the ramp, exaggerating being out of breath, to seem in a hurry.

"Hey, there," she called to the person she saw pushing a supply cart through the inner doors. "I need a ride." She clutched her side for good measure, gasped in and out a couple of times until the pilot came closer.

The light of the bay revealed their Ehrentraudian uniform, with the patch flag of the station on their upper arm, and a black stripe adorning the hem of their breast pocket. They were shorter than Katja, with a tuft of messy hair on their head and a control pad hanging off their neck. She'd say they were just an average farald, if not for the way they moved, too fluid to be a sedentary pilot, too measured to be a civilian. Yet the differences were so subtle, that Katja had to ask herself if she wasn't finding discrepancies where they weren't.

The pilot wiped their hands on their front. "Where to?"

"Medical emergency on Va." Katja pulled her cap off and fanned herself with it. "Gotta get there in eighty hours. Think you can make that?" Va was a satellite station on the outskirts of the Coalition space, in the opposite direction of any place that might host good fencers. If the pilot had indeed stolen the GEM, they'd refuse the ride.

"Sure," they said, surprising Katja. "Price is not negotiable."

"I only have four units."

"Ten."

"Come on, be a pal and help me out," Katja insisted. It wouldn't do not to try to bargain for a lower cost at least. Nobody just accepted whatever fare was requested.

"It's ten. Take it or leave it." They turned, as if to leave, and Katja decided to cut the play short.

"Fine," she said. "But you get the rest after I get paid on Va."

The pilot rolled their eyes with such undisguised long-suffering, that she briefly feared they were going to fall out of their sockets. With a wave, they gestured her in and Katja grinned.

"Welcome aboard."

"Thanks." She tucked the hat under her arm and made the universal nice-to-meet-you sign with the hand that wasn't holding her backpack. "My name's Katja Taras. What's yours?"

"You can call me Alexis."

"And what else?"

"Just Alexis."

She nodded and followed them down a hallway. "Pronouns?"

"None of your business."

"Okay, grumpy," Katja muttered, feigning irritation. "Show me where I can put my stuff."

Inside, however, she was delighted. Alexis already appeared as a contradiction, as most enby were happy to impart their set of pronouns. She studied them as they walked. Alexis had faint wrinkles at the corner of their eyes, seemed younger than Katja, but other than that, she couldn't gauge anything else.

• • •

It wasn't until she made her way to the tiny mess hall, after storing her belongings, that a thought occurred to her. Maybe Alexis wasn't actually from Ehrentraud; maybe they weren't even enby. Maybe it was a cover. In that case, if they had nefarious plans for the GEM—Katja shuddered. She had to keep an eye out, she reckoned, as she stared at the large poster on proper pronoun and honorifics etiquette glued to the wall. So far everything about the ship was standard for Ehrentraud culture, wear-and-tear notwithstanding. If it was a front, it was clever.

Alexis breezed by and slapped a meal pack on the table, not even pausing for a word. Soon after, the ship lurched forward, and then back a bit, before picking up velocity. Curiously, it didn't tremble from all joints, as Katja expected. She pulled a path-tracking sensor from her pocket and flicked it on, waiting for it to connect to her holobracelet before sticking it under the metal bench. This way she'd be able to keep track of the ship's trajectory.

She wanted to go see Alexis on the flight deck, but got turned around three times before ending up in front of her bunk door. It shouldn't have happened, not on a ship this size and not with Katja's experience. Intrigued more than ever, she slipped inside the bunk. It was time to gather some intel.

Katja started with the small room and its four beds, stacked two and two. She checked the frames and mattresses, finding nothing out of sorts. The air temperature was on a too-cold setting, but even after she dialed it up, there was a faint draft coming through. The paneling on the wall seemed well isolated, though. The metal table in the corner, with its stool screwed onto the floor, revealed no answers. Neither did the bathroom connecting the bunk to the next. The opposite door slid open without fuss when Katja pushed on the lock, and she applied the same meticulous check to the adjoining room.

It was there that she found a nameplate on the side of the table. It was mostly torn off, except for a small bit which spelled LUSIO.

What could that mean?

A search in the vessel database yielded no immediate results, so it was more likely LUSIO was part of a longer name. Storing this clue for further analysis, Katja checked the time. It was late, if one were running on the Dankmar clock. She should get some sleep, just like any reasonable medic would.

• • •

As she made her way to the mess for breakfast, Katja felt watched. But it was probably over-vigilance on her part, because Alexis stumbled in through the other door with bed hair and increased grumpiness. They didn't look awake quite yet as they pressed buttons and slammed drawers. The smell of fresh coffee invaded the room, and Katja perked up.

"Could I convince you to share that?" she asked.

Alexis grunted and threw a couple of frozen packets at her, with a vague gesture to the small oven on the other side. The domesticity of sharing meals and drinking coffee—real coffee—with a complete stranger was weird, but at the same time it felt as if they'd been doing it for years. The drink was hot and exquisitely bitter, tastier than the instant crap served on Dankmar. Speaking of which, how could Alexis even afford coffee when their ship was in such a state? It was almost as if an illusion of decay enveloped the spacecraft.

Katja's breath hitched with sudden realisation, thankfully unnoticed by Alexis. She schooled her expression into one of boredom, but was reeling on the inside.

It made sense, of course it did!

The ship was The Illusionist and its pilot the elusive thief who had managed to get away unscathed with the most controversial items in known space. The bounty for their capture was in the top dozen, still unclaimed to this day. For a decade Alexis had frustrated the best of the best and Katja held nothing but admiration for their skill.

Her fingers itched. The reward on Alexis and The Illusionist would set her for life. She wouldn't have to take another job, ever again. Her stomach flipped at the prospect.

However, it wasn't just anyone she'd be turning in. The Illusionist and its master were very popular in some circles. The ship was a symbol of sticking it to the status quo, and Alexis was the one people hired to take others down a peg—teach humility to politicians who forgot their origins, to companies exploiting their workforce. Alexis was a thief, no doubt about that, but what they stole was well aimed at the egos of deserving bastards. If Katja were asked, she'd admit to having a sort of professional crush on Alexis. Thankfully, nobody posed such questions.

Besides, there was the matter of the heist to consider.

"What're you looking at?" Alexis' voice was thick with sleep and startled Katja from her thoughts.

"Nothing, just daydreaming," she said quickly, looking down and away, faking fluster.

To be honest, it wasn't that far from the truth. Katja was in the presence of a legend. The issue was: should she arrest them, or help them? Really, it depended on their intentions toward the GEM.

Alexis sniffled and slurped more from their battered mug. Katja fought a strong desire to cool.

• • •

Katja filled the day with inconspicuously checking out the rest of the ship. If she didn't know any better, she'd have said the corridors moved, but when she looked out of the corner of her eye, she could see a mirage of well-placed holographic projections intended to confuse her.

She was thoroughly impressed, even more than before.

Alexis seemed to have disappeared somewhere, most likely to the flight deck, because Katja hadn't managed to find it. She did, however, find the cargo hold by walking through make-believe walls. The old trick with the wet finger against the draft helped.

"Take that, technology," she murmured to herself as she fiddled with the lock on the largest crate in there. It was the right size to store the GEM.

Still, it wasn't tech that kicked her ass, because the crate was empty.

Back in her bunk, she checked the path tracker, and their current trajectory wasn't even close to Va. Instead, they were gunning it straight for Ehrentraud. Katja was ninety percent convinced her assumptions were correct, but she couldn't find any evidence of the heist. Nor how Alexis had pulled it off.

• • •

Dinner was just as quiet as breakfast, and afterward, instead of trying to be sneaky, Katja followed Alexis closely. Their irritation grew visibly by the time they entered the cockpit.

"What do you want?" Alexis asked through clenched teeth.

"Just bored." Katja shrugged. "Thought maybe you'd like some company."

Alexis pinched the bridge of their nose, but gestured to the other pilot chair. Katja took a seat. She couldn't help but feel a little smug as she planned what to say to obtain the most information. It was all about satisfying her curiosity first. She'd decide what to do later.

For a while, silence sat awkwardly between them. Katja fidgeted with the zipper of her jacket, even squirmed a bit in the chair, for effect. Alexis huffed.

She stretched her legs out. "What do you think of it?"

"Of what?"

"The GEM heist."

Alexis stopped poking at the dashboard console in front of them and raised an eyebrow at Katja. "Is that what they call it? A heist?"

"What would you say it was?"

"Repossession."

The disdain bleeding into that single word supported Katja's theory. While Ehrentraudians were generally still bothered by the GEM being housed on Dankmar, Katja had heard that sharp edge in Alexis' voice only a handful of times. It was a tell of people determined to do something about whatever was upsetting them.

"Damn right," Katja said and was rewarded with a twitch of lips that could only be an aborted smile.

The new quiet between them didn't feel as uncomfortable. Alexis returned to pretend-plot their trajectory to Va.

"Why a bicycle?" she asked, leaning her head on her palm to better watch them while still maintaining a casual air.

"Hm?"

"Wouldn't gender equality better be represented by something else? Why a bicycle of all things? I would've thought non-binary people wouldn't get so hung up over an object that screams binary."

The look Alexis threw her was half flat and half filled with disbelief. "Are you serious right now?"

Katja shrugged, feigning ignorance.

"Bicycle, bi, binary," Alexis said. "That's the whole point, because a bike isn't only made of its wheels. Without the chain and the frame connecting them, motion doesn't happen. Having the two ends of a spectrum is not possible without what's in the middle, and that applies to gender as well. When the wheels are in sync, that's when we get equality, because all parts of the bike are just as important, regardless of their size."

"What about a unicycle?"

"The fact that there are many varieties of bikes is an argument pro diversity; but the GEM is about those instances when people thought there were only two ways to be, and not seeing there might be other options out there."

"Like agender."

Alexis squinted their eyes at her. Katja waved her hand in vague dismissal of her comment, as if she hadn't just pinpointed Alexis' gender—the stripe on their jacket pocket was a dead giveaway, but few outsiders were familiar with that particular tidbit.

"I see what you mean," she said. And then, because the hull of her quest for truth needed poking until the metaphorical airlock gave in, she added, "But why that particular bicycle? Just get another one and paint it over." It was so crass of her, but she needed to know for sure, once and for all, what Alexis' motivation was in stealing the GEM, if it was a paid job or something else.

Alexis stared at the screens for a while, and when they spoke, there was enough bitterness in their voice to give Katja goosebumps. "The night Ehrentraud gained independence, the entire station almost went up in a nuclear blast. One of the zealots of the Earthian council locked himself in the reactor control room and overloaded the cooling circuits before slicing his own throat." They swallowed, took a breath. "The engineer that saved us all used that bike to rush to the auxiliary control room because all the elevators and shuttles were out of power. Ze was my parent."

Alexis stood up then, and Katja thought they were going to walk off, but they flipped a switch instead. Next she knew, the straps of her chair locked around her torso and her perception of balance shattered as the room seemingly spun around itself.

Alexis landed on the ceiling gracefully, stood there watching as Katja hung upside down. She couldn't even get to the knife in her boot.

"Nice," she forced through the lump in her throat. It was never a good feeling, being caught unawares like that. "Multi-gravitational engine. Any other surprises up your sleeve?" She was both in awe and pissed at herself for letting her guard down. She'd been so focused on figuring Alexis out that she didn't notice them doing the same.

Alexis ignored her, which wasn't a good sign, but on the bright side, they didn't pull a weapon on her. Instead, Katja was regarded with a cold and calculating look that made her feel small.

"Look," she said, "I'm sorry for being an ass. I just wanted to know why you stole it. Not gonna tell anyone it was you, promise." Katja was sincere. In the light of Alexis' revelation, the decision was easy. Besides, she never wanted the bounty, she wanted the GEM back where it belonged.

"I knew you were a bounty hunter the moment we met."

Katja struggled against the straps. "Then why let me on board?"

"I needed a passenger to cover my escape and thought, who better to join me than someone smart enough to suspect me?"

That made her laugh. "Really? Well, I'm flattered. So, what now?"

Alexis sat cross-legged against the wall, and pulled a pack of gummies from their pocket. "Now you convince me to believe you."

• • •

They were at an impasse. It had been two hours and Katja needed to pee, yet still she dangled off the damn chair suspended to the floor-turned-ceiling by the inversion of the gravity field. The gummies were gone and Alexis hadn't even moved from their position. Katja's attempts at made-up explanations had all been rebuffed before she even had the chance to craft them into wonderful, juicy, intricate lies.

There was one last thing to do: tell the truth. Wasn't it ironic, though, how searching for verity in Alexis' motivations had brought her to the same endpoint? Katja sighed and rubbed at her forehead.

"Okay," she whispered. "I was born on Ehrentraud."

That particular piece of information made Alexis shift forward. "Why hide it? Are you ashamed of it?"

"No! For queerness' sake, no."

Alexis thought that over before lifting both hands. "So what? That doesn't guarantee you won't sell me to Dankmar."

Katja groaned. "Fine. I might have pondered over the size of the bounty I'd get for The Illusionist, but I came here because I was curious. I never intended to do anything that would take the GEM to Dankmar. The bastards shouldn't display it like a trophy."

"And you expect me to believe that?"

"Yeah. I was there, too, you know. That night, the kids in my school were herded into one of the nuclear shelters. That bike is important."

Leaning back against the wall, Alexis scratched at their chin. "Nis, what do you think?"

Katja's confusion was short-lived, because a disembodied voice said, "Mx. Taras is not lying. Biometric readings are steady."

She looked between the source of the sound and Alexis a few times before it clicked. "A.I. tech is banned."

Alexis smirked. "So arrest me."

• • •

Later, after she had been released and gravity returned to its usual state, after she took a long time in the bathroom to steady her circling thoughts, Katja went back to the cockpit. She could've ditched The Illusionist in an escape pod. Probably. Maybe. But she didn't want to.

"Can I see it?"

Alexis' answer was to turn a dial and push five other buttons in a pattern that seemed random but most likely was a code of sorts. With a hiss, one of the lateral panels opened to reveal the GEM.

The paint on it really did sparkle, very subtly in the dimness of the room.

Katja's chest felt tight in the face of what the bike meant, the history behind it, and the future it stood for. She formed the universal good-to-see-you sign with her fingers. When she looked at Alexis, they were smiling, small but genuine. Katja matched it.

They both took a seat, and Alexis brought up the real trajectory of the ship. "We should arrive soon."

She nodded, wondering what she'd do once on Ehrentraud. It felt so sudden, to leave, although she had no basis in wanting to stay with The Illusionist. They were complete strangers—

"So how about a job? What's your rate these days? A thousand? Two?"

Katja twisted in her chair, startled. "What? You...want me to work for you?"

"Consider this trip your interview. Congratulations, you passed. Now, there's a community of mistreated miners who'd like their land rights back. On the Earthian Moon. We will approach under the guise of mechanical failure, have a sit-down with my contact."

"Are you serious?"

"About the miners? No. We don't know yet if their claim is just."

Her breath caught in her throat in a gasp that immediately became a strangled laugh.

"Of course I'm serious about you," Alexis added.

"What makes you think I want a job?"

They turned to her, and the look in their eyes felt like it pierced all her carefully built layers. Words weren't necessary, because there it was, the cord that tied people together.

Understanding.

She held her fist up, to bump in agreement. Alexis' knuckles were cold where they touched.

It was then that Ehrentraud came into view, a speck in the vastness of space, but quickly approaching. The Illusionist was indeed faster than it appeared, and with that knowledge another thought came to the front of Katja's mind.

"How'd you do it?" At Alexis' questioning hum, she clarified. "How'd you steal the GEM?"

Alexis took a deep breath. "What do you know about teleportation?"

"That's utter nonsense."

Katja could get used to Alexis' smirk. It suited them.

So it would take longer for them to reveal their trade secrets; fortunately, she had patience. The sudden and apparent displacement of the bike from its pedestal ended with the displacement of Katja from her hunter life and into a thieving one.

She was determined to savor every bit of it.

BRIAR PATCH

Lane Fox

The path today is much smoother than I remember. Not nearly as many roots reaching up to deflect my tires. I don't have to fight the handlebars the way I did when we arrived, how long ago? More than seven seasons. Time feels strange when there are dual suns. Still, it's tempting to try to impose schedules. Find ways to link days to the world that didn't want us. Pretend the ones who left aren't exiled. Pretend there was ever a choice. As if everything we are is a choice.

I breathe deeply and fill my lungs with autumn air, spicy and crisp. The fallen leaves crunch and crackle, and I imagine their smell, like cinnamon and coriander rising in my wake. My whistling blends with the almost familiar bird song as they harmonize, friendly and unafraid.

I exult in the effort of pushing pedals, pulling the cart filled with dense sprouted breads and bagels, hard cheeses encased in wax, oils and herbs and spreads blended with love. The birds follow behind to pick up the crumbs, and I feel like Hansel or Gretel, wandering the woods, unable to find my way back to where we were.

The birds and I weave a song of thanks for everything we have while I struggle to keep it from becoming a song of sadness for what's been lost. I try to push aside the memory of my infant, pulled from my arms as I boarded the ship. It doesn't work, and the senator's name coils behind my teeth. She was there as a reelection stunt, showing how tough she was, tempered with compassion. Reminding us that if we atoned, if we chose to come back to the fold, her country would be more than willing to forgive us our tresspasses. They kept their heads down as we passed. I walked behind Tristan and Jordan, to keep an eye on them. To make sure no one got lost. Would it have changed things if I'd been first? If I'd wrapped our youngest tighter against me? If I hadn't stood tall, and proud? If I'd let it seem like they'd broken me?

She stopped us. Liked the look of the baby's curls, I guess.

I watched the news reels on the ship, after my other children were tucked into their bunks. Silent tears streaming down my face as the senator basked in the adoration of a television audience. They cheered when she claimed her prayers for a family had been answered. That she had been called to 'rescue' the child. She humbly prayed for the strength to raise her 'God-given daughter' in a home uncorrupted by the evils of unrepentant sinners.

They would be walking now. Talking. If they're anything like my other children, they'll be running headfirst through the world, knowing that it will break before they do. I send my daily dreams for them toward the sky: Be full of care, and wary of those who tell you to be careful. Please, dear child, trust yourself; trust your heart; trust that you are more than they let you be. I wipe my eyes. Swallow my sorrow. And keep pedaling.

The path turns downhill and opens into fields. I coast, head wrapped up in thoughts of who we are when there's no pattern to follow. The wonder of who I am when I'm not busy piecing myself together from scraps of what I'm supposed to be. When I can take the time to pick and choose the parts that fit the person I want to become. I'm not quite sure who that is yet, but I'm getting closer to feeling comfortable in my skin. Every decision. Every deep breath I take as I walk through the world as parent-partner-baker-maker-singer-human-me. Everything is a test; it just that now it's an essay instead of a poorly phrased multiple choice. I shift gears. The way is smooth, and I can safely speed alongside the stubs of newly harvested grains and fences of tangled, thorny vines.

I slow down as I enter town, merging with the other merchants and townspeople. I lift my hand and wave to teachers and students in the park, tending the school garden, the winter squash swollen and strange. The children adapted so quickly to the unknown, most of them eager to eat real food after the months of ship's rations. It helps that this world seems designed for us to enjoy. For dinner, they beg for the bulbous burgundy roots that grow close to the surface and smell like coconut curry when you cut them. There are broccoli-like flowers that grow in tiny Christmas tree shapes and have pollen that tastes almost like ranch dressing. They fight over the spiked pods that look like milkweed and melt like cotton candy when you crack them on your tongue.

Really, we haven't had to worry much about the food situation here. The dominant life form is mainly aquatic, and they generously gifted this continent to us. They left us guides to their favorite plants, some starter homes, and their art. At least I think it's art. We haven't been able to figure out if there's any purpose to many of the structures other than to look pretty and catch the light. The homes had to be modified a bit since they were built by creatures without bones. It was a little awkward until we cut larger doors, but the thought was nice.

I pull up to my usual stall, nodding to the candle maker to my right and the leatherworker to my left. Most people here do most things; that's the nature of new colonies. Even so, there are always those who find their hands are more adept at weaving, or growing, or carving, than their neighbors' and the market is the place to find and trade for the results of extraordinary skills. I unhook my cart, and pull my bike to the 'hitching post'. No locks. A person would sooner steal your left arm than your bicycle. Since it was easier to transport a few horses for breeding stock plus enough bicycles and parts for each colonist, we depend on our fat-tired friends for all our transportation needs. Realistically, we probably won't see horse carts or plows for another generation or so. You ask me, we do just fine with our wheels. Then again, I'm not out there plowing fields.

I set the crusty loaves on the table. The flavored oils and spices and spreads nearby. I put the wheels of cheese in the center. Those will be the first to sell. My partner's a dairy wizard, and I fell in love with their cheddar months before I worked up the courage to talk to them about anything other than food. The kids ask me to tell the story, mostly so they can laugh at my awkwardness, I think. By this point, they tend to interrupt and tell most of it themselves. They never get it quite right. So, this is my version: each week, I'd stop by their stall and linger over my choices, my heart skipping each time their hand would brush mine. I'd bring over breads to "test how they worked together." I probably bought more cheese than any reasonable family could eat. My oldest kept pushing me to do something. Say something. They reminded me that fear-fueled inaction is also a choice. And asked if it was one I was making consciously. It was...frustrating to hear my lessons being parroted back so appropriately. Then, they smirked, and jokingly threatened that they and the younger one were also fully capable of making choices about their lives, and would take matters into their own hands if I didn't "make a move." To stall, I saved the wax from the rinds and shaped it into roses. I used some of our fence vines as stems and twisted them into a lopsided bouquet. It was always "almost finished," and "not quite ready." Until, one day, it was. Nervously, I left it peeking out of their paneers after I'd packed up early on a market day. I rushed to hook my bike to my cart, my hand fumbling with the catch. I pedaled around the corner, thinking I'd wait to see their reaction. But they didn't even notice. They swung their leg up and over, and pedaled in the opposite direction.

I didn't buy any cheese the next week.

Or the week after.

The third week, I swallowed my pride and tried to talk to them again. I'm sure I blushed from toes to ears. But I did it, and I didn't die. When I got home, I unpacked my bags, and found a small selection of sharp cheeses (the kind that made my mouth water) and one of my roses.

Long story shorter, less than a month later, they'd moved in, and our booths had merged. I suppose it's the colonial version of a moving in on the second date.

It's strange to be here without them, but they're back at home, too pregnant to be comfortable riding into town for a day of bartering. Plus, they get anxious with all the friendly hands reaching toward their swollen belly. Pregnancy is strange here. Pragmatic. There are those of us who happen to have the equipment to carry babies, and those who don't. Falling in love with people doesn't always guarantee that you'll be able to blend your genetics. To be fair, there were a lot of cis people back on Earth who struggled with infertility, so I suppose that being binary and straight wasn't exactly a free pass, either.

Here, you put out a call to the community, requesting a carrier, or a sperm donor. Or you can do like some communal groups do, and keep expanding your romantic partnership circle until it includes at least one baby-making pair. It's rare that someone isn't pregnant on purpose. There's always a few requests posted near the hitching post, and I'm tempted sometimes to volunteer to carry. But not anytime soon. I remember how much work babies can be, and I know we'll have our hands full for a while. That's definitely it. The work. And not the nights I wake up with my pillow wet, and my partner's sleepy hands on my shoulder, gently pulling me from dreams of Avery being pulled from me.

I finish our display and set signs out for what we'll take in trade: Paper and paints for drawing, a few herbs and spices that we haven't been able to grow, paraffin for bike chain maintenance, and cloth for baby clothes. I sit back on the bench behind our mingled offerings, and start warming a ball of wax between my fingers, before pressing my love into each petal I craft. I've gotten better at it over the last year. Faster. Found better stems that don't droop when they're held. I suppose it might look like wasted energy. We live together now, and I could probably stop without them feeling the lack. It's not like the work will last; I know that the flowers will sit for a day, maybe two, and then be melted down, purified, and remade into cheese casings. But this is a choice I make, every day. To pour my love into small things. To remind myself that loving is worthwhile. Always.

CLASHING/COMPLEMENTARY

Rafi Kleiman

Charley tagged in four very specific places: by the chain link fence near her old middle school, at the subway stop her mom used to take to work, on the corner by her family's old apartment building, and in the dead-end brick alleyway between a warehouse and a flower shop. The latter was her favorite. The shop had a basic enchantment that kept the flowers bright longer, as well as a sign that crawled with moving vines that traced the letters.

Her mom had loved flowers. For Charley, putting her vivid purple mark on the wall and then buying one of the long-stemmed, one dollar roses by the front felt like paying homage. Charley put the rose in the living room of the apartment she shared with her father and replaced it every couple of weeks.

The flower shop was cheery and pretty and Charley didn't know who owned the brick wall she tagged, but it wasn't really attached to either of the buildings it sat between, and there weren't any cameras she could see, so she figured it wasn't a big deal. It was tucked away like a secret, because the alley had a seemingly useless turn just before the end; big, empty, beautiful brick sealed away from the public by walls that blocked the view from the street. Charley had never seen another tag there in the months she'd been doing it, almost half a year. And then, all at once, one specific tag started showing up in her space.

The first time, Charley had felt charitable. So what if there was green and gold on one of her tagging territories? Clearly someone was new to the game, and she should be forgiving, and kind. If her newest tag overlapped the other one just a little bit at the end, it was an accident. Easily deniable.

The second time, she gritted her teeth, and worked to make her purple tag as big as she could cram into the space. She hadn't brought her enchanted paint because she didn't think she'd need it today. She'd planned something small and simple, and that just wouldn't work anymore. The green and gold tag was glowing softly, low and contained like a firefly, and the only way to deal with it was to go huge. She spent much more time there than she would usually risk, planning and executing her tag so it sprawled out in twisting purple spikes across nearly the entire wall. Towards the end of her work, not quite finished, Charley heard footsteps at the mouth of the alley. Heart leaping into her throat, she pulled her hoodie over her face and bolted. She ran out the alley and away, without waiting to see if someone was actually there looking for her. To be extra safe, she skipped her usual bus stop, walking a few extra blocks to reach the next one.

Getting arrested wasn't a part of any plan that she had. Her mom might have understood that she had done it in the name of art, that graffiti wasn't any lesser for being unconventional. And then maybe Charley could have told her about how traditional art forms were fine, but if there was an artist like Charley in a museum, it was a special exhibition, not a part of the main collection. How graffiti might be Charley's only chance to see her work on a public wall. Maybe her dad would have gotten that, if she tried, for all that he didn't quite understand art. But that conversation required talking about the graffiti. And for that, Charley felt like she needed her mom.

• • •

The next time Charley went to her alley, there were no tags at all. This happened sometimes. Every so often the wall got cleaned off. In some of her other tagging spots, like by the middle school, walls got painted over with a fresh coat of beige and boring. She mostly chose spaces that weren't bothered with often—Charley didn't paint storefronts, or private homes. But getting the art cleaned up by the city was part of the ritual. It was a blank canvas. It was a new start. This time, she felt especially good about it. Balance was restored. She'd made her point. Her space was hers again.

She thought that for about a week, until she went back and saw SHARP written in green bubble letters, filled in with metallic gold and shimmering in the light. Charley sent a text to herself as a reminder to put more diverse enchantments on her paint, and got to work.

Soon, the harsh chemical scent hung in the air, and Charley gave a vindictive little smile and shook her can, hearing the distinctive rattle of spray paint. She went over the paint on the wall again, deepening the color with another layer. The can was firm and cold against the nubs of her bitten down fingernails, just a little painful on tender cuticles. When the encroaching gold and green was absolutely covered up with a fresh coat of purple, her tag done thick and heavy to block it out, she gave the brick a fond tap. There was really nothing wrong with watching paint dry. She stepped back to stare at it, waiting for the enchantment to come into effect. Her mom had taught her this one, when Charley was just old enough to try. While Charley and her dad had been cleaning out her mom's desk, just after, they had found a partly-filled notebook with ideas for more. Charley had taken it, with her dad's fervent blessing, but she hadn't added much of her own yet.

Her phone buzzed in her jean pockets, and she scooped it out and flipped it open, eyes still tracing the fresh paint.

"Hey."

"Hey, mija. Where are you? Are you going to be home for dinner?"

"Yeah, dad. I'll just be a little while longer. I'm checking something out from the library." She winced as she said it. There was a library book in her backpack from her visit earlier that day, a built-in alibi. If they were talking earlier, it would have been true; at least there was that.

A truck went by on the street behind her, and Charley pressed the phone harder to her face in the hopes that her breathing would drown it out. She picked at her nails, the phone stuck between her ear and the round curve of her shoulder.

"I'm making omelets," he said, and Charley could hear the smile in his voice.

"Well, you know how I feel about breakfast at night," Charley replied.

"You can invite a friend over, if you want. We have plenty of eggs. And cheese! I may have bought too much cheese."

"That's all right. It's a little late to invite someone for dinner." The sun was starting to sink into the city, dyeing pavement gold. There was a pause, and Charley heard water running. In her mind's eye, Charley could see her dad washing the dishes. Before her actual eyes, Charley's art seemed to solidify. The air hummed with the magic working, and she closed her eyes to lean into it, to feel it in her fingers and her blood.

"You're still looking for work?" her father asked, trying to sound so casual. Charley's ribs squeezed tight around her heart. She pressed her face against the cool brick, focusing on her magic moving so close by.

"Yeah, dad." She was, but she knew that wasn't really what he was asking. "I'll do school next year. All sorts of people take gap years. And then I'll have something saved up, for all those loans."

"You should let me worry about that," he chided. "It's my job, not yours."

"Okay," Charley said, unwilling to fight. "I should get going so I can catch the bus. I'll see you soon. Love you." She flipped her phone closed, grateful she'd escaped before he could bring up moving out, or colleges with programs that might be good for her but also might be far away, and combing through sketchbooks for something that could count as a portfolio. He'd probably ask at dinner, and she wouldn't know what to say, or how to explain, because she never did. She couldn't tell him he wasn't used to being left alone, yet. She already knew he'd tell her not to worry, and would try not to look sad.

As Charley left her alley, she shot a look over her shoulder at her tag, which was pulsing steadily, like it had a heartbeat of its own. She bought two roses that day, to replace the one that had died.

• • •

Two days later, she returned. She had never visited the alley this often when she was the only one using it. Her tag was still there. The enchantment had weakened, and now the pulse was slow enough that it was barely visible. Next to it, in letters twice as big, was SHARP in pointy green and gold, enchanted so it faded in and out rhythmically, alternating letters.

It was beautiful.

Charley was furious she hadn't done an enchantment like it before the mystery tagger did. She was also furious that the signature was done so differently than last time, willing the mystery tagger to make up their mind. Charley had decided on a tag before she even started, like you were meant to. She had practiced in notebooks and on the edges of napkins until she got it right. Charley shook her can hard, took it to the wall, felt the pre-enchanted paint stain her fingertips, and put all her spite and longing and frustration into something even bigger.

• • •

The next time she came, Charley knew something was wrong right away when she turned down the alley. The familiar acrid scent of paint was already there, and she could hear the distant hiss of a can. With all the might she could muster, Charley tried to make herself feel like more than she was, aware that she wasn't very imposing in her paint-stained old flannel and jeans ripped at the knees, dark hair braided down her back. She sped up, ran down the line of aged red brick, and rounded the corner. Kneeling in front of yet another piece, near complete, was a person with a shaved head and a pierced nose. A bicycle was propped against the far wall, scuffed and scratched all over. Charley came to a stop, pointing one accusatory finger.

"You!" The other person jumped, clapped a hand to their chest, and turned. An oversized button clipped into their plain black t-shirt said 'they/them', the letters huge on a holographic rainbow background. There was no missing that, Charley thought, annoyed by her own approval. No one who saw it could pretend they didn't know. The stranger relaxed visibly when they caught sight of Charley.

"Fucking hell, I thought you were the cops."

"You wish it was the cops! You're the one that's been painting in my space! What the fuck are you doing here?" Charley stared down at the interloper, bigger with fury than she would be otherwise, and still couldn't keep herself from saying more. "Sorry. Language. The question stands!"

"I do not wish it was the cops. Your space? It's just a wall." Comprehension dawned on their face, and they gave Charley a look that was half assessing, half sheepish. "You're the one with the purple. I was wondering."

"It's not just a wall!" Charley sputtered. "Taggers have territories—who even are you?"

"I'm Sharp," Sharp said, pointing at the word on the wall, an unfinished golden outline.

"That's your tag, that's not your name."

"Dude, I paint it on walls because it's my name."

"I am not your dude!" Charley protested, stomping one foot, and feeling sort of foolish. She couldn't let it go now, though, not after she'd made such a big deal out of it. "Why would you paint your real name on a wall where anyone could see it?"

"Well it's not my legal name. It's just my name." Sharp looked at her for a moment, their expression curious. "You really care a lot about this."

"Is there something wrong with that? I care a lot! So what! I wouldn't be breaking the law if it didn't matter to me!" Charley pulled her flannel tighter against her skin as a gust of cold wind came winding down the alley, frowning at Sharp in a way she hoped was frightening. "Why do you do it, if you don't care?"

"Dunno." Sharp shrugged. "I didn't say I don't care. But, like, I do it for fun. I'm an artist; I put my art out there. It's fun, and it pisses the cops off. I didn't realize this is, like, your area. Explains why you were painting over my shit." Charley deflated, trying to clutch the last of her self-righteous rage in her fists. She picked at her nail polish, chipping and black, watched the flake fall.

"That was kind of rude of me, I guess. Sorry."

"Eh," Sharp replied. "Doesn't really matter much. It's street art, it'll get painted over or washed away eventually anyway. I can always make more." Charley took a couple of steps closer as Sharp turned their attention back to the wall in front of them, spraying another line in green. The stud in their nose was a green gem bright against their skin.

"How did you do the enchantment from last week?" Charley blurted, eventually. "I can never get my paint to come out like that. The rhythm doesn't stick."

"Are you enchanting the paint, or the art?" Sharp asked, without turning around, lining their work in coiling green, like the vines on the storefront nearby.

"Uh, the paint? You can't just enchant the painting when it's done, that'd take way too long for one piece."

"Beg to differ." Sharp put their can down, and lined their fingers up on either side of the wet paint. It smudged, just a little, pressing into the whirls of their fingertips. "Watch." They made a face of deep concentration, worrying their brow and sucking their lower lip up against their teeth, and then exhaled all at once. Charley could feel the familiar tingle of magic being performed nearby, but that couldn't be right—Sharp hadn't said the words yet, they didn't have anything set up.

Sharp muttered to themself, something nearly indecipherable about art and light and the way the sun felt, glitter and power, and pulled one hand down to clutch at a stone hanging around their neck. Quartz, Charley thought. For amplification. The tag shimmered and then began to sway. "See?" Sharp asked. "If you do it once it's up it's more personalized, I guess? So the intention is stronger. I dunno, I've always done it like this." Charley gaped at them, impressed and also distinctly angry.

"That was too quick; you didn't even use a circle, or burn anything! How can you expect the enchantment to stay, doing it like that? Mine last for a whole week, at least. Sometimes longer."

"It's art, man. I'm not expecting it to stay. I just want it to look pretty while it's there. Maybe I'd go hardcore for a permanent piece, but this is up on someone else's wall in a public area. It'll get painted over or scratched out eventually." Charley frowned in response, thumbing at the sleeve of her shirt. She must have been just missing Sharp's comings and goings, if Charley was catching the quickie enchantments while they were active.

"I like to think we're leaving something behind," she said. "For the community. Even if it gets cleaned up every so often. Brightening things up with art."

"I don't know how much most of the community likes us painting on their stores." Sharp said, with a wry little look. "Or warehouses, or whatever. I've seen your work in the subway station though, that one's always nice. Makes the commute less boring."

"You recognized it?" Charley could feel her ears going red.

"You always use the same purple, yeah. And I think the letters are the same? I'm not sure, it's always so stylized I can't really read it. I know there's a C in there—what's your name, anyway?"

"Why should I tell you?"

"Well, I told you mine."

"But that's not a name anyone could identify you with," Charley protested. She felt silly, but couldn't seem to stop being difficult regardless. "And you're some random person I just met! You could be anyone. You could be a criminal!"

"I am a criminal," Sharp pointed out, gesturing at the painted-up walls around them. "You're a criminal too. It's not like tagging is particularly badass or threatening. I could hurt you without knowing your name, if I really wanted to, but we've just been chatting." When Charley still hesitated, Sharp got to their feet, and glanced around the alleyway. Charley felt strangely vindicated in the realization that Sharp was at least a couple inches shorter than she was, even if their tag was bigger. "Or I could come up with a name based on the tag, I guess. Is that an M? C and M. Corn muffin? I could call you Corn Muffin."

"It's not an M!"

"Well then I guess you should tell me your real name, so I have something else to call you."

"Charley," she admitted, dragging the toe of her shoe against the rough concrete. "It's Charley." "Cool," Sharp said. "Better than what I came up with."

"Do you want to shake hands?" Charley asked. "I feel like we're supposed to shake hands."

"If you don't mind me getting paint on you," Sharp said. Charley gestured at her own paint-stained clothing, and Sharp laughed, like they were surprised. "That's a point. Alright." They stepped closer, and extended their hand, and Charley grasped it, noting that Sharp's hands were bigger and a little rougher than hers. There was a smear of green on Charley's index finger when she pulled her hand back, and she looked at it for a moment. Part of her regretted that there wasn't paint on her hands that she could leave on Sharp, to make it fair.

The sound of sirens very close and two men speaking broke the comfortable quiet. Charley shot a panicked look back down the alley.

"Shit," Sharp hissed, and Charley wholeheartedly agreed.

"There's nowhere to go," Charley said, looking back and forth between the tall brick wall behind them and the cops, who had just begun down the mouth of the alley.

"Yeah, there is. You can come with me," Sharp said, and grabbed at the bicycle that was propped against the far wall. It was painted a garish lime green, and now that Charley was looking at it more carefully, what she had thought were scratches were actually sigils etched all over the surface, right into the paint. Charley recognized one of the symbols, a simplistically stylized bird, and shook her head wildly, her hands already beginning to tremble.

"No, no, no. No. I am not getting on that thing."

"It's that or explain yourself to the police," Sharp said, and handed Charley a backpack that clinked when it moved. "Put this on." Charley did, even while she continued shaking her head.

"Is it even licensed? Do you even have helmets?"

"Hah, no," Sharp said. "And just one." They leaned in, and clipped a shiny silver helmet onto Charley's head, her braid pressing uncomfortably into her scalp.

"I am not running away from the police on your illegal bicycle!"

"You're already painting illegally on buildings! What's the difference?"

"A bigger fine!" Charley hissed, shooting a panicked look down the alley, peeking out from behind the wall that shielded them. "I can't afford that!" The cops were significantly closer. They may not have been able to see them yet, down in the curve at the end of the alleyway, but it wouldn't be long. Sharp swung their legs onto the bicycle, ignoring the pedals entirely but gripping the handles. They were so far forward that they straddled the frame, leaving almost the entirety of the bike seat behind them free. For her, Charley realized. They were leaving space for Charley.

"You won't get fined at all if we don't get fucking caught," Sharp said, and, well. Charley never had a hard time fighting when she wanted to, but she didn't have any reasonable response to that. With one last nervous glance towards the sound of the approaching cops, Charley clambered up onto the bike, Sharp's backpack swinging with her. "Okay, now put your arms around me," Sharp said, urgent, and Charley couldn't bring herself to argue. She wrapped her arms around Sharp's waist, her hands interlocked against the soft heat of their stomach. Sharp tensed in concentration, muttering under their breath. "Up, up. Come on you piece of shit, I don't have time for this right now. I don't want to get you out of impound."

The bike lurched a couple of feet into the air, not high enough to make the wall.

"Oh god," Charley said, her whole body tight with fear.

"Come on, come on, come on," Sharp coaxed, like their bicycle was a frightened cat in a tree.

"Get down from there!" a voice behind them yelled, and Charley gripped tight to Sharp and squeezed her eyes shut. She pressed her face into the back of Sharp's neck, praying they were far enough away that it couldn't be seen. The bike made a whirring noise, the wheels spinning with nothing beneath them, and then shot up higher. Charley squeaked when she felt the wind go past her ears. She squeezed her arms tighter around Sharp's stomach, earning a half-hearted "oof" from them.

"Don't look down," Sharp said.

"Why would you say that?" Charley asked, her eyes snapping open. "Now all I can think about is—Oh, oh gods." The ground was very far below them, but somehow not far enough, because the cops were hurrying back to their own vehicle. "They're going to chase us."

"They can't chase us. They'd look ridiculous. Imagine the headlines; two coppers drive after a pair of young people on a flying bicycle and lose them."

"We haven't lost them yet!" Charley insisted, and her voice came out very high in her throat. "Drive, come on, you've got to know how to do more than go up!"

"Okay, okay, hold on." The bicycle began to speed forward, staying level as it did. Sharp's fingers were white-knuckled on the handlebars, but the bike was being held upright by its own power, not attached to either rider with rope or clenched thighs.

"They're following us- Sharp, if we don't lose them we can't come down!"

"Okay, okay, calm down! I'm on it!" Sharp snapped, tension in their voice. "The yelling isn't exactly helping, Charley."

"Sorry," Charley said, her voice almost lost in the wind. "I just—I can't believe I'm in a police chase. I can't believe this is happening."

"Escape now," Sharp said. "Process later." The bike made a sickening right turn, wobbling slightly in the air as it tipped them sideways, and Charley squeezed her eyes shut again. It was still holding itself in the right place, but how long could that last?

"Oh gods, oh gods," Charley repeated, under her breath. The police car roared to life below them, following as they flew above the city streets. Sharp dodged an oncoming power line, and Charley felt herself nearly overbalance. She locked her legs into the bike's frame and held on tighter, her hands fisted in Sharp's t-shirt. She could feel every inch of Sharp's big black backpack on her spine, bumping up against her as they moved. From below them came the sound of sirens, and then a loud, incongruous roar. Charley looked over her shoulder, her stomach twisting at the view, just in time to see the police car push off the ground.

"Sharp—" Charley started, but Sharp was already nodding.

"I saw. Shit," said Sharp. "The one traffic patrol in the city with flying permissions. Of course, of fucking course." They leaned forward, and the bicycle tipped with them, heading downwards. Charley readjusted her arms around Sharp's waist, closing her eyes against the rush of wind as the ground jolted towards them, putting a fence between them and the police car that could do absolutely nothing to keep them away now that they were in the air. "Okay!" Sharp yelled over the noise. "The way I figure it, we're smaller and stupider than they are! We just have to go somewhere they can't follow!"

Charley scanned the road for a lifeline as they flew down it, despite the ice settling in her stomach. The green bicycle's wheels spun freely beneath them, though the pedals stayed still. Charley knew the streets here, full of weird nooks and crannies and shortcuts she had used when she was in high school. There had to be something. Her vision caught on a narrow back alley with a shadowed, gaping mouth. A piled-high dumpster had been wedged in front of the walls, unable to fit any further down the alleyway. Charley leaned in closer to reach Sharp's pierced ear.

"There, go left!" Charley risked pulling one of her hands off of Sharp's waist to point, wobbling in her seat. "We can go through the alleys, they won't fit! They can go above, but maybe if we're fast enough, they won't know which way we went!"

"Gotcha," Sharp replied, and promptly turned right. "Uh. I didn't mention. It doesn't go left. I haven't figured that bit out yet."

"Oh for the love of-" Charley twisted her fingers into the hem of Sharp's shirt. She was probably stretching it out, but she couldn't seem to care, not right now. She'd feel bad later. "Turn right two more times!"

Sharp turned, and turned again, and the world went wonky in front of Charley's eyes. Trash bags dragged under Charley's dangling sneakers as they cleared the dumpster, and then picked up speed. They soared down the narrow back roads, faster than their pursuers could follow, though here there was no space to turn again and again for one left. The walls were close on either side of them, scratching at Charley's shirtsleeves, but she couldn't mind when they were so much closer to the ground, now. She urged Sharp and their bike through skinny streets and back behind businesses. They wound their way through the back roads until the sirens faded, and then they did it some more, pushing the bicycle fast enough that the wind rang in their ears and the sound of their pursuers was like a distant memory.

"Where should we touch down?" Sharp asked, when it seemed very nearly safe.

"A few more streets," Charley answered, and turned to make sure there was nothing worrying at their backs. "Somewhere near a bus line." The two of them hovered past buildings and street signs, and finally Sharp took them down in a nearly deserted neighborhood park. They parked their bicycle behind a tree in an attempt at the most subtlety one could get with a bright green flying bicycle and vaulted off it while Charley stumbled on weak legs, leaning against the trunk.

Sharp began to laugh, loud and breathless like they couldn't stop themself. The park was lonely and painted with long shadows, sun aching to set. Charley looked at Sharp to find them grinning at her with their fingers still tensed at their sides, not quite fearless, and Charley cracked a smile back. "That was terrifying."

"It absolutely was, but what a goddamn rush! We did it!" Sharp kicked the parking break down on the bicycle, to give it a well-deserved rest, and ducked in to kiss Charley on the cheek. Charley felt her face burn, and hoped it looked like adrenaline. "Thank you! You saved my ass! Both our asses!" Sharp pulled back, holding themself at a hovering distance as they looked for more to say. "And, uh, you can give my backpack to me now." It took Charley a minute to remember she was holding it.

"Oh. Right." Charley handed it over. Her shoulders had begun to ache, now that they were safely on the ground. So had her legs. "What's in there, anyway? It's really heavy." She picked at her nail polish, and pushed out her last words in a rush, before they could fly away. "And I couldn't have saved anything if you hadn't saved me first, by letting me on your horrible green deathtrap. So. Thank you."

"Me and my deathtrap say you're welcome," Sharp replied, their smile still broad. "And it's paint. Mostly, anyway. Couldn't hold it and still have you behind me, you know? Especially with steering. We probably would've fallen off and died. Thanks for that."

"What, for not letting us die by holding your paint?"

"That and navigating. I probably would've kept on heading right. I'm not used to flying yet. This baby's pretty new." They tapped their nails against the board, beaming. "That wasn't half bad, for a trial run."

"You hadn't used it before?" Charley asked, her eyebrows shooting up to her hairline.

"Not like that!" Sharp replied, bouncing on their toes. Charley took a shaky breath, and reminded herself that she hadn't bashed her brains out on the pavement and died, even if she had apparently been very close.

"I guess you're right, then. That it wasn't half bad. Thank you again. For, you know. Not leaving me to get arrested or whatever."

"Well, I'm not a total asshole," Sharp replied, with a laugh. "And like I said, I would've fallen or gotten caught without you."

They bit their lower lip, and Charley looked away, fiddling with the embroidery on her jean pockets. "So, uh." Sharp started speaking again, and Charley's head shot right up to meet their eyes. "Before you head out. For your bus. Any chance of seeing you again sometime? Maybe on the ground this time, with less cops involved?"

"Yeah, actually," Charley said. "Sure. We can get something to eat or whatever. Talk about what else we do. You can show me how you did that quickie enchantment on your tag. Even if you don't want it to last, that was way fast." Charley fished in her pockets and pulled out her phone, an old-fashioned flip. "Don't laugh at me. Just put your number in."

Sharp took it, chuckling. "Man, this thing is ancient."

"I said not to laugh!" Charley said. She tried to frown, but it wouldn't come. Sharp handed the phone back, a new contact still up on the screen.

"Okay, now you text me and I'll have yours." Sharp grinned. "I can walk you to the bus stop, if you wanted. Or," They nodded towards their bike, their eyes sparkling. "I could just drive you home."

"I am not ever getting back on that thing!" Charley took a big step away from the bike, and a little closer to Sharp. "At least not until I know you better!" She thumbed out a quick message to Sharp's number, glancing up at them from behind her bangs. Her mouth quirked into a smile, and Sharp smiled back, holding their phone in hand like they were just waiting for it to go off. "But I guess you can walk me. And maybe I'll consider asking you over for dinner, if you've got nothing else going on. But only if you promise to keep at least one foot on the ground at all times."

"Cross my heart," Sharp said, and they did.

LUCY DOESN'T GET ANGRY

Tucker Lieberman

She had reached the age when she was old enough to know what the elders planned for her but was still too young to prevent it. Every now and again, the elders sacrificed a child to the Minotaur. It was her people's custom. They delivered the child to the beast's Labyrinth and locked the gate, sealing the child inside. Alone on the morning she was to make that walk, knowing nowhere else to go, she crept away to the edge of the village and approached the Centaur's Woods to seek his advice.

A bronze bell, tied to a tree branch by a green satin ribbon, was at her eye level. She rang the bell. The leaves shimmered alive in the summer air. High in the forest crown, a bird chirped. The Centaur appeared, his hoof striking a large root with a thud.

The Centaur's horse body was velvety chestnut brown. Under the moving shadows of the trees, light seemed to sink into his fur without reflecting. His human half rose from the horse front, a muscled abdomen and chest showing through an unbuttoned shirt. The shirt's purple and gray flannel wrapped his shoulders without hiding their strength. The girl lifted her head higher and saw the dark eyes of his wise, kind face set by dark hair pulled back.

"I'm Sequoia," the Centaur said.

"I'm Lucy," the girl said.

"I know," said the Centaur, raising his eyebrows. A stray acorn cap fell from his hair and landed between his front hooves and her gray sneakers. "For now, you are Lucy. But it's your Sacrifice Day."

"I don't want to be sacrificed. Can you tell me what to do?"

"I can't stop you from going in, if that's what you're here to ask me about. Terribly sorry. I hope you're not angry with me."

Lucy sighed. "I don't really get angry. I just need to know what to do."

He folded his arms. "Your Sacrifice Day is when someone else chooses for you to enter a Labyrinth. If you want to start making your own choices, you have to know what to do."

"Do you know what I have to do?"

"Yes. I have a certain feeling about you."

"But you won't tell me?"

"No. You have to feel it yourself. Come." He turned. His horsehair had been braided into thin ropes that were then wound around the wooden handle of an axe, and his weaponized tail swung menacingly from side to side as he walked. Lucy followed from a careful distance.

At the edge of a clearing, the Centaur gestured with his right human hand. Lucy saw a bicycle leaning against a tree.

"Take this," he said, bending to strum the spokes of the wheel with his finger. The wheel spun; the gear purred. "And this." Moving some paces away, he swung his axe tail at a tree and lopped off a low-hanging branch. He handed the stick to Lucy. "Your weapon."

She looked at the stick without emotion. It smelled of sap. She placed it under her arm.

"Can I bring both of these into the Labyrinth?" she asked, touching the dusty blue metal of the bicycle.

"Yes, you must. Now you must go. It is time for you to fulfill your quest. Meanwhile, I have an appointment to watch the people who travel to and fro among the stars. I am sorry I cannot be of further use to you. Oh, by the way—watch your anger."

She wasn't angry. Was that a problem? All her life she'd known she might be sacrificed. That wasn't her choice any more than the name given to her at birth. The ordeal she was facing now was a destiny that had always seemed written for her. She had long felt resigned, even though now as the final moment drew near it was natural for her to resist. Most children did. She'd heard wails and seen struggles as the gatekeeper locked the previous victims inside and the elders watched impassively. She was ready to resist too, in her own way. It depended on what she must do. This bicycle, this stick; she could use these tools. Could she feel angry?

"Wait, Sequoia."

But he was gone.

• • •

"No one said I couldn't bring anything." Lucy stood before the opening of the Labyrinth, the staff that Sequoia gave her secured in a knapsack, the blue bicycle leaning on her left hip.

"Very well," the Labyrinth gatekeeper sniffed. "You have a right to fight and flight. Don't expect it to make a difference, though."

A high wall circled the Labyrinth. Lucy moved toward it and passed through the cavelike door. The crowd watched her silently. The gatekeeper slammed the iron bars behind her. She heard the door lock.

The maze was tight. Left, right, left, right, left. She walked the bicycle because she couldn't ride it around the corners. Would the bicycle be any use if she needed to escape the way she had come in? Right, left, right, left, right?

She had thought it would take longer to—well, to end things. To encounter whatever it was, this Minotaur, at the center of the Labyrinth. And perhaps she had thought that it would hunt her, that it would find her by her scent, that it would gloat over her first before she realized the game was over.

But no, she smelled it first. As she pressed on, its odor grew stronger, until the air resembled a cattle pasture. She pulled the stick from her knapsack and placed it across the handlebars of the bicycle. She began to hear the Minotaur's breath like the hum of a motor. Then, turning a corner, she saw it. The corridor had opened up into a giant room with no roof, a room that was empty except for old, dry fingerbones on the floor and the hulking, smelly beast brooding over them. Its back was to her.

Could she strike the Minotaur in the back and wound it? She needed to believe. Now was her moment.

As she raised the stick, the beast turned. The Minotaur was mostly naked. His loincloth was splashed with sticky, brown blood. He had a pulsating gland in his chest. The wishingstone, Lucy thought.

The Minotaur bared his pointed, curved teeth. Lucy lifted the bicycle off the ground and held it like a shield across her chest, preparing to throw it to distract the beast.

"Give me that," said the Minotaur.

"No!" she yelped, uncertain what she should do next.

"Give me that," he said slowly, "and I will give you something you want."

"No." Her arms began to tremble with the weight of the bike. She was consumed by the jangle of her own fear, manifesting more and more of its own energy, mixing up hopes and hatreds. She couldn't think of anything in particular she really wanted. All she could think about was iterations of Minotaur and Labyrinth, nothing else.

"Make a wish. Wish for anything you want." The wishingstone pulsated in the beast's chest. "But choose carefully. And then give me the bicycle."

"OK," Lucy said. She put the bicycle down. She thought about what she needed. To live, she needed to defeat this beast. But how? She didn't know. Only the beast knew. More than anything else, before she took another step, she needed his perspective. She confessed her need: "I wish I knew what you know."

The Minotaur nodded solemnly. "Roll it here."

She balanced the bike upright and gave it a shove toward the beast. It rolled in the Minotaur's direction, and he caught it with a click of his long fingernails.

"Very good. You'll find that the transfer is complete. So, tell me," he said, "what do you know now?"

She reflected a moment. Her response tumbled out in words she didn't understand, like a half-remembered poem. "A girl needs to be a boy like a Minotaur needs a bicycle." As soon as the words left her tongue, she began to feel what they meant.

"That's right," the beast said sadly. "I need this bicycle very much. Let me show you how I ride."

He mounted the bicycle with some difficulty. It seemed that his huge, bull-headed body should crush the child's bike, yet, once on it, he balanced as if he were lighter than air. He placed his feet on the pedals and began to circle the great room under the last rays of sunlight. He gained speed, pedaling faster and faster, circling Lucy. She held the stick Sequoia had given her in both hands.

Lucy knew more than she had yet admitted. She realized she knew everything the Minotaur knew. He was made of anger. Her anger. He was her anger riding her bicycle. It wasn't fair. It wasn't right.

"I will not be inside you," she said.

He let go a sort of beastly giggle—loud, chesty, gleeful—still pedaling in circles around her.

"I am not inside you," she said. "I don't know who you think I am, but I am leaving your Labyrinth. This is my Sacrifice Day, and I get to decide what I give up. I am already gone."

As the Minotaur reached his highest velocity, Lucy threw the centaur-split stick at the bicycle wheel. It caught in the spokes and stopped the bicycle short. The Minotaur lurched over the handlebars and flew over the walls of the Labyrinth. There was a long silence. She didn't hear him fall to the ground. He was vanished.

All that effort, she thought, to make such a powerful thing and then to erase it.

But she had taken its knowledge. Among the things she knew:

She could see her anger and separate herself from it.

She could be a boy if she wished.

A girl needs to be a boy like anger needs to move.

He could use that anger if he wanted.

He knew his way out of the Labyrinth.

He could make it hard—pretending he did not know how to exit, riding his old bicycle around corners to go back the way he had come in, right, left, right, left, right, returning to a former life—or he could make it easy. He had the Minotaur knowledge.

"I choose the easy way," he said aloud to himself.

Just then, he noticed a door in the wall. It was engraved "Lucy" at his own eye-level and was covered in dirt and ivy. He brushed away some of the dirt and saw more of the etching. The word wasn't "Lucy," after all. It was "Easy."

He pushed and the door did not move.

He pulled and the door did not move.

With his newfound anger that bubbled up in a quick, hot burst, he hit the door with both fists. The door fell off its hinges and hit the ground like a drawbridge, leading him to the outside. He was out of the Labyrinth.

He had been willing to sacrifice something, but he wouldn't let himself be eaten today. He wasn't that Lucy. It was that easy.

BEYOND

Nathan Alling Long

The slim volume, *A Theory of Gender Relativity*, ultimately changed both the fields of astrophysics and gender studies, and it took someone like Madeline Stein to develop it. "M'ine'Stein," as she came to be known as, had observed that the faster a population moves in time and space—using cars and planes and bullet trains—the more fluid their gender expression becomes. She posited, then, that as one approaches the speed of light, just as matter turns into pure energy, humans turn into a pure, genderless state.

Initially the theory was laughed at, as many great accomplishments of humankind are. But a hundred years later, when Djune Arrappe took the first bicycle into space and came back half the man they were—which is to say, twice the woman, or rather, neither the this or the that—feminists and physicists began to nod their heads in agreement with Stein's general theory.

From that, the great Race Beyond Gender was born—a grueling but exciting interplanetary romp that let one transform until one felt completely comfortable with their non-gendered body—and built up a good deal of calf muscle in the process.

Even back in the 1900s, it was well known that the bicycle was the most efficient mode of human transportation for energy expelled. Once the oxygen recycler and solar food transformer were developed, it wasn't long before the first velostation orbited the earth.

It was from this station that the Race Beyond was launched. There were over a hundred brave adults—and a couple of teens—who took the challenge to pedal from Earth to Pluto and back, daring to come back, exhausted, but transformed.

They said goodbye to their loved ones, or their scowling families—and took off. The crowds at the station and down on Earth cheered.

The final push from Earth's gravitational pull was tough—a few dropped out in the first few hundred kilometers of the thermosphere, and two broke down just into the exosphere and gave up. But 99 pushed on, picking up speed in the void, with the help of solar winds and solar panels.

The news of the race was on the tel-al every hour for the first few days. As it was not actually a race, they did not report the names of those in front—in fact it was well expected that many would change their names by the end of the race anyway, and there was no telling when that might happen.

Along the way were a dozen rest stations with spare parts and tools, beds, real Earth-grown food and meteor-mined water, and call stations to report back home. But, it turned out that few called home. One rider, who called themself Rider X, kept a telablog, writing of how the Earth kept changing as it became a shrinking dot on the spherical horizon. "Whatever change I go through is nothing like that change," X wrote. "I grew up in Kansas and never knew anything but the land below my feet, and now I can't even find that land half the time when I look for it in the sky."

“I’m still going to come back human, but the Earth is never going to be the same,” wrote another rider.

As they passed Jupiter and Saturn, Earth heard less and less from the 99, but could track them by interplanetary satellite. “Still picking up speed” wrote one rider; “Tired,” said another when interviewed.

Rider X wrote only once a week now, short phrases and comments.

“Gender in space is like weather in space.”

“You have to leave the planet to understand that there is no day or night. Everything just is, is, is.”

“I’m nothing. Feeling fortunate to be able to experience that.”

A giant Half-Way party was planned for the 99 on Pluto, and as they approached, knowing the crowds that would be on the surface, the riders started speaking again, not with elation, but with fear.

When Pluto was still a speck, one of them wrote that “it looked crowded down there,” and another said, “All that land, like a blotch in the sky.”

“Ninety-nine riders spread out over 500 kilometers in an endless void was starting to feel crowded enough,” said one rider who called home at four in the morning, having lost all sense of time. “What season are you in?” they even asked, before saying they had to go.

Then activity on the private inter-rider communicators began to increase, and conversations with Earth and its stations ceased. The front riders held back, letting the back riders catch up. They were just a few days ride now from Pluto, almost halfway through the race. They seemed to want to come down all at once, make a grand entrance, people speculated. Crowds started watching the group again on the tel-al.

And then, they shocked the worlds by just pedaling right past the planet, beyond the last outpost of humankind. The crowds on Pluto stared up and gawked, their streamers limp in their hands. The newscasters, having prepared to announce the arrival of the great 99, were speechless.

All attempts to contact the riders failed. But before the last satellite connection was lost, Rider X wrote a final teleblog entry.

"We are not who we were. Neither are you. Do not worry about us. Follow us. Good night."

BIOGRAPHIES

Charlie Jane Anders is the author of *Victories Greater Than Death*, the first book in a young adult trilogy, which comes out in April 2021. She's writing a series of essays about how to use creative writing to survive hard times, over at Tor.com. And she's the co-host of the podcast *Our Opinions Are Correct*.

Ava Kelly is an engineer with a deep passion for stories, especially those dedicated to trope subversion, those that give the void a voice, and those which spawn worlds of their own. Their novel Havesskadi is currently available from LT3 Press, and their holiday-themed Snow Globes series has been published by Nine Star Press. Find them and their works at www.avakellyfiction.com

Juliet Kemp lives in London with their partners, child, and dog. Their fantasy novel "The Deep And Shining Dark" (Elsewhen Press) and their YA SF novella "A Glimmer Of Silver" (Book Smugglers) both came out in 2018. They can be found on Twitter at @julietk.

Rafi Kleiman is a gay, Jewish writer in a committed relationship with both urban fantasy and media diversity. They think it's incredibly important that people of all types can see themselves reflected in the art they consume in varied, respectful, and well-researched ways. They spend much of their time thinking about mermaids that can actually kill people, and can be found on Twitter @mothmanlives.

Lane Fox is a former teacher, diesel mechanic, long distance runner, waitress. Current rugby and roller derby player, parent, partner, living in Germany. Occasional writer, artist, clown. Future therapist. Analog/gender queer. They/them pronouns.

Tucker Lieberman is the author of *Painting Dragons* and *Bad Fire*. His poems are in Defenestration, Déraciné, Esthetic Apostle, Gingerbread House, Oddball, Prometheus Dreaming, and Rockvale Review; his fiction in Owl Canyon's *No Bars and a Dead Battery* (2018) and DefCon One's *I Didn't Break the Lamp* (2019); and his essays in anthologies including the 2011 Lambda winner *Balancing on the Mechitza: Transgender in Jewish Community* and the 2012 Lambda nominee *Letters for My Brothers: Transitional Wisdom in Retrospect*. In middle school, he wore a dress on the MacNeill/Lehrer NewsHour to read a haiku and was congratulated by U.S. Poet Laureate Rita Dove. Today he lives as a man. He studied at Brown University and Boston University and trained as a life coach at the Easton Mountain gay men's retreat center in New York. He lives with his husband, the science fiction writer Arturo Serrano, in Bogotá, Colombia. www.tuckerlieberman.com

Nathan Alling Long grew up in rural Maryland, lived on a queer commune in Tennessee, and now lives in Philadelphia. Nathan's work appears on NPR and in various publications, include Tin House, Glimmer Train, Strange Tales V, and Impact, a Queer Science Fiction anthology. The Origin of Doubt, a collection of fifty short fictions was released Spring 2018 by Press 53.

Ether Nepenthes is a queer, non-binary, disabled writer hailing from the south of France. They have already published as part of UNBURIED FABLES, a collection of fairy tales with a queer retelling (Creative Aces, 2016), TRANSFORMATIONS, an anthology benefitting Trans Lifeline (Carnation Books, 2019), and SPECULATIVE MASCULINITIES, an anthology exploring masculinity in speculative fiction (Galli Books, release to be announced). Find them on Twitter and Tumblr @overlaured.

Lydia Rogue is a writer and poet living in Portland, Oregon. They write stories and nonfiction that centers trans people, when they're not writing sappy love poems for their spouse or wrangling their four rats. You can find them online at lydiarogue.com

M. Darusha Wehm is the Nebula Award-nominated and Sir Julius Vogel Award-winning author of the interactive fiction game *The Martian Job*, as well as seven science fiction and five mainstream novels, several poems, and many short stories. Originally from Canada, Darusha currently lives in Wellington, New Zealand after spending several years sailing the Pacific. Find out more at darusha.ca

Marcus Woodman is a gay, transgender man born and living in Lincoln, Nebraska. He typically writes fantasy, but all his stories are unabashedly queer. More of his works can be found on orcishreject.wordpress.com.